BLOOD SECRETS

THE WOLF BORN TRILOGY

JEN L. GREY

CHAPTER ONE

My heart raced as we pulled onto a narrow road to Lillith and Katherine's vampire nest. Even though the two vampires had become close friends of mine and Roxy's at Kortright University, I wasn't sure how their family would react to everything. I'd be squirming with concern if it hadn't been for Donovan's head on my lap and his injured body sprawled across the seat in the back row. I asked, "Is your nest similar to you?"

"Meaning, do they drink straight from the human and kill?" Lillith's dark brown eyes reflected in the mirror. It was late, but her dark makeup and eyeliner were still intact, contrasting against her pale skin and almost matching her black hair and all-black clothing.

"Well, yeah." I wouldn't lie to them. It wouldn't do any good. Everyone would smell the lie. My focus went back to my mate, who was barely alive beside me. Even though we'd killed the evil vampire, she'd drained him and his best friend, Axel, so much that their survival was barely plausible. Roxy and my only choice had been to bite them and hope they survived the transition.

I ran my fingers through Donovan's short jet-black hair and gently brushed his cheek. His dark stubble scraped my hand. His skin was warm like he had a fever; the transition was still underway. Or I hoped the fever was due to the change. The other consideration I couldn't bear. I needed to see his gorgeous, bedroom blue eyes soon.

My rose-gold hair fell over my shoulder and blocked a portion of his face. I lifted my blood-tinged hands and pushed my hair behind my ear. I could feel the deep circles under my light blue eyes. They were a few shades lighter than his.

"Yes, all the members are focused on retaining their humanity," Katherine reassured me and turned to face our group in the back. She'd pulled her long, dark brown hair into a ponytail, and I could see her brown eyes, which were almost as dark as Lillith's. The concern was clear on her face.

"How much longer until we get there?" Roxy complained as she stretched. She'd been stuck, sitting on the floorboard between the two middle row seats since Axel needed to recline. He was just as injured as Donovan and also undergoing the change, and there was no way in hell Egan could fit anywhere else but in the other chair. She'd kept her hand on Axel's leg the entire time, needing to touch him for reassurance.

"About five minutes," Lillith replied curtly. "We have to go down the road a ways."

"God." Roxy shook her head, her bright red hair brushing my legs with each movement. "I'm not sure I can make it much longer."

Egan's slight accent made his words sound rough as he said, "That comment isn't appropriate right now." His whole body stiffened. He wasn't fat by any means, but he was huge. He looked like a can of biscuits in the chair. Blood had crusted on his arm from where the vampire had ripped scales off his body, and dark circles lined his golden eyes. His normally styled, longish blond hair was in disarray, but the worst part was that he smelled of burnt skin from the vampire he'd blazed. He rubbed the blond stubble on his chin. "Axel's and Donovan's lives are teetering, and I can barely breathe without cramping, but I'm not complaining. They have it much worse."

"You don't think I know my mate's life is hanging in the balance?" Roxy snapped, narrowing her hazel eyes at him. "This whole situation sucks ass."

I loved how eloquent my best friend always proved to be. "Everyone needs to calm down. All our nerves are frayed." I touched Roxy's shoulder. "Just focus on the fact that their hearts are still beating and we're getting more distance from my dad."

It was crazy. I was now an alpha in my own right. Granted, it was only a pack of two—me and Roxy—but I was an alpha, nonetheless. If the two guys made it, our pack would increase to four. Dad had never thought I'd be an alpha because I was a girl and weak, but here I stood. I pushed away the fact it had only happened as a means to survive. It didn't matter. I was officially responsible for Roxy's safety.

"You're right." She scooted back and rested her head on my legs. "It's just ... I don't see how we can survive long-term."

I didn't either. Dad was the strongest alpha out there, and he had his sights set on becoming king over all supernaturals. It was absurd, but our family had been building this legacy for years. My great grandfather had built most of the supernatural neighborhoods and businesses in the world.

Having another supernatural in charge meant they didn't have to hide what they were or what rooms they needed and why. But what they hadn't anticipated was that my family would have all of the blueprints and knowledge on how to take down ninety percent of the population if need be. There weren't many places we could run and hide. "How long has your neighborhood been established?"

"It's not a neighborhood." Katherine licked her lips and checked her phone. "It's about ten acres of land with one huge house on it."

"So, my family didn't build it?" Could we be so lucky?

"Nope. That's one reason your dad shouldn't be able to find us." Lillith kept her focus on the road. "We stay off the grid for several reasons."

I wanted to push for more information, but I dropped it.

Donovan groaned, pulling my attention to him. He jerked his head from side to side as if he was having a bad dream.

"We're almost there." Katherine pointed to a huge mansion about a mile away. It was a symmetrical, three-story, brick building. A large red door sat in the middle with a few brick steps leading to it. "Just hold on tight."

"Holy shit, you weren't kidding when you said it was a large house." Roxy's mouth dropped. "How many bedrooms?"

"Fifteen with sixteen full bathrooms." Lillith flew down the dirt road, leaving a cloud of dust behind us. "Don't worry. We have plenty of room for clothes and enough space that we won't want to kill each other."

"What clothes?" Roxy sighed, and tugged at her Kortright sweats.

Donovan's jerking intensified as we pulled up to the house. His arms thrashed, and he groaned in pain.

"Guys, something's wrong." I'd almost thought this would end okay, but this reaction couldn't be good.

"What's wrong?" Egan asked as he tried to turn around to see in the backseat.

"I don't know, but he's thrashing around." I tried to keep the hysteria from my voice, but I failed miserably.

"We're here." Lillith drove through the grass and pulled right up at the front door. "Let's get him out."

"Should I be concerned or relieved that Axel isn't doing that?" Roxy straightened, careful not to hit her head on the car ceiling.

"I'm not sure," Egan said. He opened the sliding door to the van and jumped out. "I'll go get Axel while you two pull Donovan out."

Lillith hurried over to Axel and opened the side door.

"Okay." Roxy turned around, her forehead creased with worry. "Let's do this."

Right as she reached for Donovan, he began to flail around, and he punched her in the face.

"What the hell?" she grumbled and grabbed her nose. "Damn, that hurt."

"Come on." We had to get him out of here and get him in a bed or on the floor. Something better than a damn cramped backseat.

"Fine." She grabbed his feet and tugged them toward the middle row. His body slid awkwardly, and I snagged his arms, trying to hold them in place despite his wild movements.

Roxy struggled and dropped his feet on the floorboard, jarring his body even harder.

Loud noises came from outside, but I couldn't even pretend to listen. For all I knew, Egan was getting attacked and sucked dry. The only reason I didn't flip out was because I trusted Lillith and Katherine to protect us, which I hoped I didn't regret.

"Move, Roxy," Egan commanded. He climbed through the door on Axel's side. "I'll help her."

"Thank God." She hurried out the other side of the van and rushed inside to find Axel.

"Once we get outside, I'll carry him in like Axel," he said and secured his legs, taking some weight off me.

We slowly moved out of the van, making sure we didn't drop Donovan. It was no easy task. He was built like a freaking linebacker, and even though Egan was larger, the dragon struggled as well.

Egan stepped out of the car and swept his arms under Donovan's legs. "Got him."

Any other time, I'd have died laughing at seeing Donovan being carried away like a princess on her wedding night. He wasn't doing well, and his body shook even harder than it had inside the van.

"Sadie!" Roxy screamed with terror from inside the house.

My stomach dropped. I rushed behind Egan, and we hurried up the brick steps and inside the mansion. He ran down a long hallway that opened to a huge living room. Two L-shaped leather couches sat across from each other.

Eight vampires stood around, watching Roxy lean over a convulsing Axel

"What do I do?" Roxy looked at me like I held all the answers.

"I don't know." I pointed to Donovan as Egan laid him on the other couch. "Donovan is doing the same thing." She already knew that, but I tried not to snap at her. We were both scared that our mates wouldn't make it out of this alive.

"What the hell is going on?" A man who had to be in his

late fifties marched over and slid the large wooden coffee table out of the way. His hair was almost the same shade as Lillith's, and his eyes were brown with a slight red hue laced through. He was close to my height but slender like most vampires tended to be.

Lillith nibbled on her lip. "The humans were almost drained."

"Almost drained humans don't act like this ..." He trailed off and took a deep breath. "And they don't smell human."

"Are they being turned?" A woman similar in age to the older guy placed a hand on her chest. Her face had the same sharp angles as Lillith's, but her eyes were a lighter brown, and her hair was dirty blonde. "Please tell me you had nothing to do with it?"

"No, I didn't." Lillith stared at the ground, her usually confident demeanor gone. "But we got into a situation."

Donovan's body took on a life of its own as his shivering turned into convulsions.

"He's seizing." A petite middle-aged woman with light blonde hair ran over to us. "You do realize they probably won't survive this."

"Oh God, no!" Roxy cried as she leaned over Axel. "They have to."

I didn't have time to deal with all this negativity. I needed to do whatever I could for Donovan. "What do we do?"

He began foaming at the mouth, and his body shook so hard it rattled the couch.

"Someone fetch a thick washcloth!" the blonde lady yelled. "Otherwise, he'll bite his tongue off."

"I'll get it." Katherine blurred across the room, going God knew where.

"Axel needs one too!" Roxy yelled. "He's shaking harder too." Her voice cracked through the pain.

The one thing I hadn't expected as alpha was that I would feel her hurt more strongly than before. The fact that I could feel her emotions more vividly worsened my pain. I channeled not only my own hysteria but hers too.

"Hold his head, and I'll hold his arms," Egan said and locked Axel down so he couldn't thrash as much. "Maybe if we calm him down, he won't be as bad off as Donovan."

"Katherine, get your ass in here!" the blonde lady called as she grabbed Donovan's head. "You," she said, glancing at me, "hold his arms like that guy's doing over there. The less rocking he does, the less likely he'll injure himself."

"We should give him more vampire blood." Lillith bit into her wrist. "Wouldn't that heal him faster?"

"Wait ... you gave them your blood after they'd bitten them?" The older man turned and glared at her. "No wonder they're convulsing."

"What do you mean?" I was missing a crucial piece of the puzzle.

"What Cassius is saying is that giving them vampire blood after you injected them with wolf saliva was a terrible mistake." The blonde girl hissed and held on to Donovan's head tighter. "The wolf genes are trying to take over, and their wolves are trying to connect with their bodies. However, the vampire blood is preventing the connection. When vampire blood heals a wound, it congeals around it. The wolf can't affix itself to the skin and penetrate the blood. It's like the two sides are colliding."

"Are you saying he might turn into both?" The vampire transition was easier, and more people survived it, but it was still damn hard. The transition into a wolf had less than a one percent survival rate, and the ones who survived usually developed a disability. That was why wolves tried not to change anyone.

"No, I'm not." Cassius arched an eyebrow. "Unless the vampires injected them with their venom."

"I didn't do that, Dad." Lillith sighed. "I'm not stupid."

"Then what are you saying?" Roxy's voice rose even higher.

Katherine entered the room with the washcloths.

"The wolf side is trying to take hold, but the vampire blood is the problem." The blonde woman snatched a cloth and tossed it to me. "I'll open his mouth, and you shove it in." She glanced over her shoulder. "Katherine, go do the same for that guy."

"On it." Katherine hurried over and followed the instructions.

Both guys were still convulsing, but then their heartbeats increased rapidly.

"Why is that happening?" Their racing hearts petrified me.

"Their bodies are fighting." Cassius dashed over to Axel. "They're trying to change."

"Can we help them?" Egan asked, his usual calm demeanor fracturing.

"Pray," the older lady responded.

That didn't sound very promising.

Their hearts picked up speed until I couldn't tell where one beat ended and the other began. It sounded like a freight train running down the tracks.

Then, both hearts just stopped.

CHAPTER TWO

My ears had to be deceiving me. "No." I pushed the vampire out of my way and stood over my mate. I might feel bad about it later, but right now, I didn't give a rat's ass. "Donovan." Tears flooded my eyes until I could barely see. "You can't leave me."

Roxy's wail filled the air, commingling with mine. We'd lost our mates in the blink of an eye and all because of my father.

"Dammit, Donovan." I compressed his chest, needing him to come back. With each push, I lost hope; however, it drove the next compression harder than the last. I'd do anything—give anything to bring him back.

I lowered my mouth to his and blew air in hard, filling his lungs. I'd do CPR until my arms gave out.

"Sadie ..." Lillith whispered and reached for me, but I shoved her away.

"He's not dead." He couldn't be. My world began to crumble, and I refused to allow her to look at me that way. He wasn't a lost cause. "You'll see."

"Girl ..." she started, but I turned my back to her and went back to helping my mate.

As I pressed down again, a steady heartbeat pounded in my ears. Was I imagining it? Could it be possible? I leaned down and pressed my ear to his chest, and each pump grew stronger.

"Roxy, is Axel's heart beating?" Please, God, don't let this be my imagination gone wild. Hope spread like wildfire through my veins, and if I was wrong, I wasn't sure I'd ever be the same.

"It is," she exclaimed. "Axel!" Then I heard her pounding on his chest.

My knees hit the ground. I hadn't realized the toll that nearly losing Donovan and Axel had taken on me. My hands shook, but I touched his arm, needing to feel his warmth.

"How is that possible?" Cassius's face turned a shade paler. "Their hearts stopped. I heard it."

The blonde woman walked over to the other side of the couch and leaned over. "The slightly sweet smell of vampire blood is gone. Maybe the wolf fought off the blood."

Donovan's eyes fluttered open, and my world stood still. For those few agonizing seconds, I'd thought I'd never see them again.

I focused on the sound of his and Axel's breathing and beating hearts. I'd never heard such wonderful sounds before. We'd come too close to losing them.

"What the ..." Donovan trailed off and glanced around. "Where am I?"

"You're at Lillith and Katherine's home." I tried to keep my voice level to hide my anxiety. There was no telling what would happen or what issues he might have. But his surviving the change was the most important part of the equation.

"Hold on." He sat straight up and took in the room. "A woman bit me ..." His head turned to Axel, and he threw his legs over the edge of the couch. "And she went after him next. Is he okay?" Before he could stand, his head wobbled, and he fell back against the couch.

"He's fine. Slow down." I kept hold of his arm, needing him to acclimate to his shifter form before standing. "You've both been through a lot." I wanted to cry with relief, but that would only freak them out even more. I had to hold it together.

Axel shifted to sitting up and moaned. "No kidding," Axel grumbled. "Roxy, are you okay?"

"You almost died." She wrapped her arms around his neck and buried her face in his buzzed brown hair. "So, no, I'm not okay."

Her emotions flooded me. They were the same as mine, making it more difficult for me to keep myself in check. *Don't overwhelm them. They're going to feel enough as is.*

You're right. She didn't budge from him. *But I need a second.*

I couldn't fault her for that. I wanted to wrap my arms around Donovan and never let him go. Hell, my wolf howled, wanting to do the same thing. The bond between us was growing stronger, and it had to be because he was all wolf now.

"Wow, this might have all been worth it." Axel paused before returning her embrace. "But what the hell happened, and why do I feel different?"

"We will leave you alone to talk." The older lady smiled and motioned for the others to follow.

"I still don't understand." The blonde woman obeyed

but looked at Axel and Donovan again. "They shouldn't have survived."

"Survived what?" Axel asked with trepidation.

The vampires scurried out of the room, leaving Egan, Donovan, Roxy, Axel, and me alone. Egan stood awkwardly in the middle of the room but didn't budge.

He must not have wanted to be alone with all the vampires. I didn't blame him. Shifters felt more comfortable around each other.

Donovan blinked, adjusting to his surroundings. "What happened to us?"

"You were attacked by a vampire." They were full wolf shifters now; I could smell their musky scents. Thankfully, Donovan's scent still hinted of rain, which comforted me. At least he hadn't completely changed.

"Is this a sick joke?" Axel laughed, the corners of his brown eyes crinkling, but he stopped when no one else joined in. "You're kidding, right?" He was the smallest out of the three men but larger than the average human. From what I could gather, he had some wolf in his bloodline as well.

"No, she's not." Donovan ran a hand through his hair and blew out a breath. "I remember now. It was the same girl who tried to get Chad to help her that night we were at the restaurant together. That was why you ran after him, isn't it?"

"Yeah." There was no reason to lie. "She had already killed the hostess and was going after her next meal."

"And you didn't think to tell me?" Donovan glared at me. "You didn't think it was relevant?"

"I was protecting you." That was what I had been doing the entire time. "That was why I kept pushing you away."

"A lot of good it did us." He snickered without humor

and focused on Egan. "And what are you? A wolf, too, since you're here with us?"

Egan scratched the back of his neck. "Not exactly."

"Then, please," Donovan said, his tone tight, "enlighten us to what the fuck you are."

"You need to calm down." Egan stood in front of Donovan and crossed his arms. "I get that you're angry and confused, but we helped you. You need to remember that."

"Oh, so we should thank you?" Donovan rubbed his temples as anger charged between us.

"You believe all this?" Axel released Roxy and leaned back, but he pressed his hand to his head. "I think there's something wrong with my head. My vision has changed."

"Mine too, and I feel funny." Donovan scowled at me. "What did you all do?"

"You remember how I told you that you're part wolf?" Maybe if I downplayed it, he wouldn't freak out as much.

His eyes darkened to a navy blue as he remembered. It had been right before we'd had sex, partially completing the mate bond between us. "Yes."

"Well, I had to bite you." I could feel Axel's and Donovan's turmoil through the alpha bond. Axel was more confused and shocked, and Donovan's emotions were strong, but I couldn't pinpoint how. Sure, the anger rang clear, but there was another emotion I couldn't put my finger on. Like fear, but not quite. "And now you aren't a partial wolf." I tried not to wince, but I couldn't help it. "You're now a full one like me."

"And what about me?" Axel's brows furrowed. "Why am I here?"

"Because I bit you." Roxy clenched her teeth. "You were going to die if we didn't change you."

"Is that why I feel so different?" Axel's mouth dropped.

"I'm a wolf, but why do I still look human?" He glanced down and patted his penis, then his legs, like he was making sure they were still there.

"Because you're a wolf shifter." Roxy grinned despite the situation. "You're part human too."

"You didn't tell him anything, did you?" I was a little surprised. They were close, and I figured Donovan would have confided in his best friend.

"Didn't have time." Donovan tensed and glared at me. "After I left you, I went back to the dorm. Your little douchebag buddy came knocking and said you were in trouble in the woods right outside the library." He closed his eyes and shook his head. "There wasn't any hesitation. I took off."

"And I followed him, telling him he was insane. I told him if you were in trouble, would that snobby-ass really tell us?" Axel rubbed a hand down his face. "God, I feel dizzy."

"It'll get better," Roxy reassured him, but it fell short when the air took on the sulfur smell of a lie.

"What the hell is that?" He waved his hand in front of his nose. "It smells like rotten eggs or horrible gas."

"I did not fart," Roxy said indignantly.

Leave it to her to digress from the conversation.

Egan must have been on the same page as me because he steered the conversation away from gas. "And the vampire was waiting for you?"

"Actually, no." Donovan pinched the bridge of his nose. "We got there, and I couldn't find you anywhere." His attention came back to me. "I freaked out, but then I heard screams deeper in the woods."

"She lured you to that spot, didn't she?" Dammit, I shouldn't have taken a nap while all of this had been going down. I should've realized Dad would do something. This was all my fault.

"Apparently so." He leaned back on the couch, and his shoulders sagged. "When we got to her, she ran so fast she blurred, and before I knew it, her teeth had sunk into my neck."

"I tried to get her off him, but after a few seconds, she turned on me." Axel shivered. "But it was insane. When she bit into my neck, it didn't hurt."

"No, it's not supposed to be traumatic unless they want it to be." Or that was what I'd been told. At least, she hadn't wanted them to feel pain, just wanted to end them. The only suffering she'd hoped to inflict was on my end.

"Then I got dizzy." Axel touched his neck. "There aren't any bite marks."

Egan sat on the other side of the couch Donovan and I were on and said, "It's because you've been healed."

"How is that possible?" Donovan touched his neck too, checking for bite marks. "Wolf shifters don't get injured?"

"We do, but we heal quickly." Right now, it was best to leave out the little detail that they had ingested vampire blood. One issue at a time.

"How did you find us?" Donovan asked.

"The vampire had attacked me earlier." I glanced at my leg, knowing my wound had already healed. "We were already on high alert. Katherine and Lillith were staking out the dorm. I'm not sure how you got out without them seeing you."

"Because Brock told us your Dad was in front and to sneak out the back." Donovan huffed. "Of course, it was all a damn lie."

"He didn't want the vampires to see you." Egan shook his head. "We should've accounted for that."

"Wait..." Axel lifted a hand. "You're saying your two buddies are vampires. The same kind that almost drained me and Donovan dry? Weren't they just here a second ago?"

"They aren't like the one that attacked you." I hoped these were the right words needed to reassure them. Lillith and Katherine had tried to protect them the same way we had. "They helped get you two out of there and someplace safe."

"Speaking of which." Donovan glanced around the room. "Where the hell are we?"

"Somewhere in the Smoky Mountains." I couldn't be more specific because I didn't even know where exactly. "We're with their family."

"We're in a house with a bunch of vampires?" Axel took Roxy's hand. "Are we sure that's smart?"

"It's fine." Roxy linked with me. *Right?*

They wouldn't have brought us here only to kill us. I had to believe that reasoning. I wasn't worried about our two friends, and for them to have such strong morals, their nest had to be the same way. Vampires were easily corrupted. That was one reason why Dad had forced our vampire friends to hunt Donovan and Axel down in the woods. He'd been hoping their vampire instincts would take over once they smelled the human blood. Even though they had in a way, Katherine and Lillith had been strong. They'd stayed away when the slightest temptation had set in.

"We've gotta get back to Kortright." Donovan tensed. "We have class tomorrow."

"There's no going back," Egan said, saving me from having to deliver the bad news. "If we take one step on campus, Sadie's dad will descend on us. There will be no saving you a second time."

"How long do we have to stay away?" Axel fidgeted. "We can't fall behind."

"For a while." Egan met my gaze. "Sadie's dad is looking for us. We might not even go back this semester."

"Then we go back and take them out." Donovan stood and slowly walked around the room. His breathing increased. He was obviously not pleased. "Easy-peasy."

"You don't understand." They didn't know how our world worked. "My dad has power and influence. We can't just take him out with our small group here."

"Do you realize how damn hard I've worked to get into that college?" Donovan turned, his anger funneling right at me. "Despite hopping from school to school, Axel and I busted our asses to make sure we didn't get behind. We want a better life for ourselves."

"I'm sorry." I walked over to him and reached for him. "I didn't mean for any of this to happen." The last thing I wanted was for him to give up on his dreams or change his life because of me. "But we have to come up with a good plan before we go back."

He moved, preventing me from touching him.

"Hey, man." Axel climbed to his feet and glanced at his friend. "Look, I get that this isn't ideal, but they are helping us."

Out of everything he could've said or done, Axel stood on our side. He'd been fighting Roxy and me the entire time, but now he was the most reasonable of the two.

"Maybe, but everything we worked for has gone down the crapper." Donovan headed down the hallway to the front door.

"I'm sorry." I hated that he was struggling.

"Yeah, you've said that already." Donovan exhaled, and

his eyes softened ever so slightly. "I need some air." He turned and walked out the door, leaving me behind.

CHAPTER THREE

E verything inside me screamed at me to follow him, but he needed space from me. By following him, I'd be disrespecting his wishes.

Axel stepped toward the door and almost fell over. "This will take some getting used to."

"Is it really that different?" Roxy's eyes twinkled with interest. "I thought you'd be steadier on your feet."

"No, it's off-putting." He looked around the room. "It's like everything is in 5D."

Egan lifted an eyebrow. "I don't think 5D is a thing."

"Exactly." Axel pointed at him. "That's what I'm getting at. It's like everything is more dimensional and sharper."

"I can help you," Roxy said and stood. "I don't want you to get hurt."

"Thanks, but I need to talk to Donovan." Axel brushed his fingers along her arm. "He needs to talk to someone, and I'm the only one who understands what he's going through."

"If that's the case, why aren't you upset and angry?" I was thankful that whatever animosity had been brewing between Axel and her seemed to be gone, but I'd expected him to act more like Donovan was. Donovan and I were pretty much mates now except for the official claiming part.

"I'm thankful not to be dead, and the three of you have everything to do with that." Axel shrugged and glanced at Roxy. "And if this is why you fought against being with me so hard, then now, maybe we can be together."

"But Donovan and I didn't fight nearly as hard, so you'd think it would be easier for him to accept." Maybe by turning, he no longer felt a connection with me. Could it be possible? Had I somehow ripped his side of the mate connection away by biting him?

"Donovan was damn determined to be with you. I was scared. That was the difference." Axel took steadier steps toward the front door. "It's going to be okay. Just give us a few minutes."

As he opened the door, Egan called, "If anything happens, all you need to do is yell."

"I've really messed up." My shoulders sagged, and I plopped down on the couch. I wanted to wallow in self-pity, but now wasn't the time.

"Hey." Roxy sat next to me, taking my hand in hers. "Donovan has always been very focused and doesn't like things out of his control. He just needs time."

I wasn't too sure about that. I might have messed up but leaving him to die hadn't been a viable option. At least, he was alive to reject me. It'd be easier to know he'd left me and was happy than for him to be a rotting corpse in the ground. "Maybe." I didn't want to hear any more false sincerities. They didn't smell like lies because they believed it, but they couldn't know.

Katherine entered the room and asked, "Is everyone okay?"

"Define okay." Roxy frowned at me.

Lillith and the rest of the vampires entered right behind her.

"That's fair." Lillith nodded and sat on the couch across from us. "I take it Donovan is less than thrilled."

"That's one way of putting it." Egan turned his attention to the unfamiliar vampires. "Is this all of you, or are there more around?"

"Nope, this is all of us." Cassius stepped in front, taking the lead. "How about you? Will any other dragons be making an appearance?"

It was obvious that he was the head of the family.

"Not as of now." Egan crossed his arms and leaned back. "Unless we need reinforcements."

"Yes, Katherine and Lillith told us what's going on." Cassius's attention landed on me. "They informed us that you're Alpha Tyler's daughter."

"I am." It physically hurt to admit, but the truth was supposed to. "But I'm no longer part of his pack."

"They told us that part too." Cassius straightened his shoulders. "That's the only reason we've allowed you to stay here."

Roxy rolled her eyes and scooted next to me. "Wow, and I thought Lillith was tactless."

I loved that she was protecting me even though we were outnumbered and had no clue where we were.

"It's clear you know all about us." A vein in Egan's neck bulged. "And that we're at a disadvantage."

Egan was very secretive and liked to hold his cards close. I'd never seen him this rattled, but they knew more about us than we did about them. It had to put him on edge, especially since I wasn't exactly comfortable.

"I wouldn't go that far, what with you being in our

home, which is supposed to be hidden." Cassius cut his eyes to Lillith and sighed. "But at least, you are safe."

"This is my dad," Lillith said, pointing at Cassius, and then she motioned to the older woman with dirty blonde hair. "And my mom, Dawn."

"Those are your parents?" I hadn't been expecting her to call her sire that. "I mean ... that's an odd way of putting it."

She chuckled. "No, they're actually my parents. We were born vampires."

Those were rare. The more supernaturals I met, the stranger this all became. "That's not normal."

"And hanging around a dragon is?" Dawn smiled kindly at me.

"True." Vampires weren't immortal like in the movies, but they aged very slowly once they hit their twenties. "But I thought born vampires were rare and ..." How did I say *evil* without insulting the very people keeping us safe —for now?

"Our family has always been odd." Cassius puffed his chest. "We're one of the original bloodlines and haven't been tainted by the vampires who turned after us. Becoming a vampire is a gift that many have taken for granted."

The room fell silent as we processed that bit of information.

"And this is my mom, Julie." Katherine placed her hand on the woman with light blonde hair who'd been attempting to help me with Donovan. Then she looped her arm through the arm of the man on her other side. "And my dad, Paul."

The middle-aged man grinned with adoration at his daughter, warming his pale face. He had the same dark brown hair as his daughter, but his eyes were more gray than brown. "Katherine has told us plenty about you. It's a pleasure to meet you."

"Are all of you vampire born, then?" Egan asked, his body becoming more rigid.

Paul gestured to Lillith's family. "No, we were turned by them about ten years ago."

If they'd turned these people, they couldn't be as good as we had originally thought.

"They were in a house fire, and we helped them." Lillith cleared her throat, reading my thoughts. "They almost burned to death. We got to them too late to save them, but they begged us to do whatever we could to help them live on. I'd always wanted a sister." Lillith averted her gaze from mine as if she was ashamed.

"And we didn't drink from them," Dawn reassured us. "We only bit them to inject the venom."

"What about those two?" Roxy pointed at the two younger male vampires behind the group. One looked a few years older than us while the other looked younger.

"Those are my brothers." Katherine turned her head toward them. "The younger one is Luther." She gestured to the one on the left who looked almost identical to her. The only difference was that he had five inches on her. "And that's Athan." She pointed at the older one. He looked like an even combination of their parents with his father's gray eyes and his mother's light blonde hair. "Athan was visiting from college when it happened."

I wasn't sure whether I should say I was sorry or not. They all looked well acclimated, even though Katherine's two brothers gave us a wide berth.

"I'm surprised those two are already up and walking around." Dawn crossed the room and peeked out the window. "From what I gathered, most newly turned wolves can barely function, especially with whatever disability results from the change."

Whatever they were, I had a feeling Donovan might hate me now.

"They may not." Egan wiggled in his seat. "They were partial wolves, so it's not like a full-blooded human getting changed."

"Really?" Cassius's head tilted back in surprise. "How do you figure that?"

"Their eyes glowed at times." In those moments, I'd gotten completely lost in his eyes. "And Roxy is Axel's mate while Donovan is mine." How I wished I could say I was Donovan's, but I wasn't so sure anymore.

The front door opened, and Axel entered the room. The corners of his eyes crinkled. "Sadie, you need to go out there and talk to him." His tone held an edge.

I jumped to my feet. "Is everything okay?"

"Well, I don't know." Axel inhaled sharply, and his nose wrinkled. "What's that super sweet smell?"

"It's the vampires." Roxy patted the spot I'd just vacated beside her. "They smell sweet to hide their cruel and vicious natures."

"Is she serious?" Athan asked with disbelief.

"Just ignore her." Lillith waved a hand at my redheaded bestie. "She projects her self-hatred onto others."

"Please." Roxy huffed. "There is nothing to hate about myself."

Even though I enjoyed their banter, tonight was the exception. I was exhausted and heartbroken, and their carefree joking grated on my nerves. "I'll go check on Donovan."

"He refused to talk to me, so I hope you have better

luck." Axel grimaced as if that nugget of information pained him to admit.

Yeah, I doubted that. "We'll see." I forced my legs forward, and my hand shook as I reached for the doorknob. I hated leaving Egan, Axel, and Roxy alone with the vampires, but they didn't give off any threatening vibes.

The outside air had a chill. It was early October, and we were high in the mountains. Temperatures like these were the most comforting. It was hard for a shifter to get cold, and so coolness always felt amazing against our blazing-hot skin.

The crisp mountain air filled my nose. It wasn't polluted like the cities we lived in. Yes, we always lived out in suburbia, but it didn't come close to smelling this pure.

I stepped off the porch and caught Donovan's scent. I sniffed and followed his signature smell toward the woods. I didn't like him being out here alone, this far from the house, but it wasn't like I could get on him about it. He was a grown man, for God's sake.

I stepped into the woods and heard him breathing. He couldn't be more than a hundred yards away.

The trees grew denser, and squirrels scurried through the branches. A few owls hooted close by, and when I glanced up, the moon seemed much closer than it usually did. It almost felt like the world had stopped moving.

When I passed a large oak tree, I found Donovan sitting on a log, staring up at the night sky.

There was enough room for me to sit next to him, but I wasn't confident enough to do it. I'd always felt insecure around my father, but right now, there was no comparison.

"I take it Axel sent you." Donovan kept his focus upward, but he'd acknowledged my presence.

"Yeah, but if you want me to leave, I can." I closed my eyes and steadied myself for his rejection. It'd hurt, but he deserved to process this in his own time. His whole life had changed in the past three hours.

"Look, I get I'm being a prick." He nibbled his bottom lip. "But I'm so angry."

I could empathize with that. I remained silent, letting him say whatever he needed to.

"I worked my ass off to get to that school." He stretched his legs out in front of him. "And now, it's just thrown away because monsters exist. How did I not know about this before?"

"Our kind ..." I started, and he winced.

"God, I hate the way that sounds," he spat. "Our kind ... I'm supposed to be human."

That stung. "The supernatural races are kept secret from humans." If I wasn't too specific, maybe he'd stay calm.

"Why?" He caught my eye. "So they can be prey?"

The problem was, I again couldn't discern what he was feeling. It was like a bomb of emotions exploding inside him. "That's not fair, and you're stereotyping."

"Oh, did that offend you?" He placed a hand on his chest. "I apologize."

"I get that you're pissed, confused, and whatever else you want to throw in there." Dad had treated me like nothing my entire life, and I refused to let anyone else do that. That cycle ended here and now. "But if you talk to me like that one more time, I'll make sure you don't ever do it again."

"What?" Donovan leaned away from me. "You going to bite me again?"

He might as well have kicked me in the gut. "Really? That's how this is going to be between us?"

He didn't answer me, just leaned his head back to look at the sky again.

"You do realize if I hadn't bitten you, you'd be dead right now." He wanted to mourn and think about all the things he was going to miss out on. "You can go back to college when it's over. You can still live."

"With an animal inside me." He huffed. "I can't chance hurting someone."

"Your wolf has been there the entire time." I closed the distance between us and stood in front of him. "This isn't a brand-new thing."

"Maybe, but it's brushing against my mind." His jaw clenched. "And it feels as if it could surge forward at any time."

It was because they hadn't been acquainted yet, and he needed to get his emotions in check before he turned. If he shifted now, he might not be able to shift back to his human form. "You will gain control of it. And wolves aren't like vampires. They don't have to feed off humans to survive."

"Maybe not, but your dad sure doesn't have an issue with harming people." Donovan crossed his arms and looked disgusted. "I'm thinking wolves aren't as innocent as you're making them out to be."

He had me there. Dad would hurt anyone who got in his way. Hell, he'd be looking for us now that I'd turned my back on him. He had no heir and no leverage to handpick the next alpha over his pack. "There are good supernaturals just like there are good humans."

"And let me guess, you're one of the good ones?" he asked mockingly, and I'd had enough.

CHAPTER FOUR

"You know what?" I took a menacing step toward him. "I'm trying to be understanding, but this is where I draw the line. I get that you didn't ask for this, but a little respect goes a long way. Turning you was the only way to save you."

His shoulders sagged, and he shook his head. "You're right." He looked at me with remorse. "I'm sorry. It's just, I like control. I haven't had a lot of it most of my life. Now that we're finally out of the system ... my future was finally in my hands. And I lost it all in one night."

"You can't actually be in control of your life." Destiny always had her plans. "It's a nice concept, but it's not possible."

"Maybe, but I feel like I'm back in foster care." He fisted his hands. "Once again, a decision was made for me that I had no say in."

"It's not like I could have asked." If he was trying to make me feel bad about what I'd done, it wouldn't work. Being alive trumped the alternative. "You were unconscious. Would you have said no?"

"No, I wouldn't have." He hung his head. "You did the right thing, but dammit, it's like I can't make my own path."

Humans loved the idea of free will. It was something they held dear to their hearts and one thing we supernaturals didn't get. Good people had bad things happen to them, and on the flip side, bad people had good things. It made no sense how they could believe in free will when it was obvious there were other influences woven into their lives ... into their existence. Destiny wasn't fair. "There are things out of our control."

"Obviously." He pinched the bridge of his nose. "And I'm taking it out on you, which isn't right."

"Then why are you?" If I didn't put my foot down and stop him from using me as a punching bag, he'd think he could do it from here on out. "I wasn't trying to rip everything away from you."

"I know that." He patted the spot next to him. "It's messed up, but I can feel how much you care about me. I never had a chance to lash out before, and I'm being a complete selfish ass. But this connection between us petrifies me. It's like the icing on the freak-out cake."

"Freak-out cake?" I felt his remorse, which softened me some. "Really?"

"Oh, stop." He took my hand in his. "But is it normal? To feel so drawn to you."

"Yeah, that's how fated mates are." Thank God he still felt our connection. I wasn't sure how I could have survived if he'd moved on and left me behind. "You felt part of the tug since you were a partial wolf, but now that you're whole ..."

"I thought it was strong before, but this ..." He scooted closer to me. "It scares me."

"Partially, it's because we had sex." Our mate bond was

pretty much firmly attached, but we hadn't claimed each other for everyone to know we were taken. It was probably a good thing because, if he was struggling now, then us completing our bond would make things harder on him. "Our bond is pretty much intact, and then you got changed, so it's more intense than it was a week ago."

"Pretty much intact?" His brows furrowed. "What do you mean?"

"For it to be officially sealed, we have to claim each other." It felt good talking to him like this. Our wolves intermingled, and he wasn't overflowing with anger.

"How do we claim each other? What the hell does that mean?"

"It just means we bite each other and our scents intermingle." It probably sounded so weird to him. Hopefully, he wouldn't freak out again. "That alerts all other shifters that we're off the market."

"But you bit me," Donovan said with confusion. "Doesn't that count?"

"No, not really." My cheeks were growing warm, which was stupid. "It has to be consensual and is followed by cementing the bond. Most couples that bypass a ceremony do it during sex. It's way more intimate that way."

"Oh, okay." He turned his body toward me. "Why didn't you tell me that earlier?"

"Because you'd just found out you were part wolf, and I didn't want to scare you away." Now that I said that, it sounded a little crazy. Instead, I'd bitten him and turned him into a full-blown wolf. "I had hoped to ease you into it."

"That plan went out the window." He dropped my hand, and his body stiffened. "And I dragged Axel along with me."

"You're blaming yourself for Axel getting turned?"

"Yeah. He's my best friend, and I dragged him into this mess." His jaw clenched, and he glanced at the ground. "He'll hate me when it's over."

"He isn't freaking out like you are." With all of the other emotions running wild, maybe that was the feeling I couldn't put my finger on: self-loathing. "I'm thinking he'll be just fine."

"I'm not so sure." He yawned and sagged a little.

"Let's head back." I stood and tugged him to his feet. "We all need some sleep. It's been a very long night, and it's almost dawn."

"Okay," he said and followed me toward the house.

Inside the house, everyone was still sitting in the living room. We introduced Donovan to everyone, and Lillith guided us to our rooms. Egan had a room to himself while Roxy insisted she and Axel stay together. All of our wolves were volatile and needed to be with their mates.

Make sure you don't do anything hasty. Warning her to not rush their relationship was important. *He's still acclimating. Don't do anything to make it worse.*

Fine. She pouted as they entered their bedroom and closed the door.

I turned to Donovan. "You don't have to stay with me if you don't want to. We can have separate rooms." I purposely didn't mind link with him, not wanting to scare him.

"Nope, we're in it together." He entered the bedroom across from Roxy and Axel's, tugging me behind him.

The room was large with off-white walls. A wrought iron, king-sized bed sat in the center, covered with light blue sheets. Nightstands sat on either side of the bed and a large, matching chest of drawers stood against the opposite wall. At the foot of the bed, a huge flat-screen television was mounted to the wall. To the left were two large windows that overlooked the woods. It gave a sense of isolation and, dare I hoped, peace. Along the side wall, a door led to the bathroom.

"Do you guys need anything?" Lillith asked from the doorway.

"No, I think I'm just going to sleep in these clothes." That reminded me. "Is there a store nearby?"

"Yeah, we can run into town." She took a step back into the hallway. "If you're good, I'm going to crash. It's been ..." She trailed off as if searching for the right word.

"Rough?" I suggested.

"That's one way of putting it." She tapped her fingers against her side. "Okay, I'll see you in a few hours." She closed the door, leaving me and Donovan alone.

I crawled into bed, and Donovan followed suit. He pulled me into his arms and kissed my lips. I responded, enjoying the feel, especially after one hell of a night. Even though I'd have loved to do a lot more with him, I was exhausted.

He chuckled and booped my nose. "Let's get you some sleep." He brushed his lips across mine before cuddling me in his arms. I was out cold within seconds.

———

THE NEXT MORNING, I woke up to an empty bed. I reached over and felt his pillow. It was cool. He'd been gone for a little while.

Had he left in the middle of the night? Maybe I'd read him wrong and he'd snuck away at the first opportunity. I jumped to my feet, my heart pounding, and ran down the hallway. *Roxy, where are you?*

It's about damn time you woke up, she chastised. *We got tired of waiting around and went out into the woods.*

They aren't ready to shift. If they shifted without getting their emotions under control, we could be in a world of hurt. *Please tell me they aren't.* I didn't think I'd ever been this stressed out in my life. Turning Donovan had made me more insecure than ever before.

I know. They're still in human form, she said comfortingly. *We're just walking around the woods. That's it.*

Okay, I'm on my way. I rushed down the stairs and followed their scents to the kitchen. The kitchen was huge with so many white cabinets running along the wall that I couldn't easily count, and they framed an electric stove right in the center with a double oven. A gray island contained a sink in the middle of a breakfast bar with four barstools.

The dark gray countertop complemented the cabinets and island perfectly as did the dark oak floor.

"There's Sleeping Beauty." Lillith snorted, drawing my attention to the large, rectangular oak table she sat at with Katherine and Egan. The dragon sat at the end of the table with an almost finished plate of pancakes and bacon. Lillith sat facing me, her back to the window, and Katherine glanced over her shoulder and smiled. They both held clear glasses full of blood.

Here, they didn't have to hide what they ate.

"How long has everyone been up?" I glanced at the clock on the black stove and saw that it was almost noon. "None of us went to bed till four."

"About an hour or so." Egan took a bite of his food. "Your pack is already out."

"Yeah, that's where I'm heading." My eyes flicked to the biscuits and bacon on the stove. "Who made breakfast?" My stomach growled.

"Mom." Katherine smiled. "She missed making breakfast and ran out this morning to get food for you all. There's plenty if you want some."

"Thank you." I walked over, grabbed a biscuit, and filled it with a handful of bacon. "I'm going to go hunt those three down. There's no telling what Roxy might be up to." I loved the girl, but she could be unpredictable at times.

"That's a good idea." Egan grabbed his water and took a large sip. "I'm trying to give those two time to adjust to being wolf shifters and not freak them out with my dragon."

"Smart idea." I grinned. "But it wouldn't hurt if you came out there with us. Donovan knows you, and anything familiar might do him some good."

"Yeah, okay." He crammed the last bite of food into his mouth and stood.

"What about us?" Lillith pointed to her drink. "We're almost done."

"I'm thinking since a vampire nearly drained them, we need to give them a couple more hours before you tag along." I wasn't trying to be a bitch, but hell, if my introduction to the vampire race had been with psycho bitch, I wouldn't be thrilled with the race either.

"If we pressure them, they may never trust us." Katherine reached across the table and patted Lillith's hand. "You have to admit it was traumatic last night."

"Yeah, but we helped them." Lillith pouted. "And let's head into town at some point today. I'm dying to go shopping. There's this small boutique that has amazing clothes."

"We do need clothes." I went to the glass door that opened up to the woods from the kitchen. "Let me see what they're up to, and maybe we can head out soon."

"Now that sounds like a plan." Lillith bared her teeth at

me. "If those two newbies have a problem with it, tell them they might find vampire teeth in their necks again."

"No." Egan closed his eyes, but the corners of his mouth tipped upward. "We will not tell them that."

Sometimes, it was scary how similar Roxy and Lillith were. "I agree with Egan. And don't worry, it won't come to that. Even if you and Roxy have to go into town alone."

"As long as it's her and not you." Lillith glanced at my clothes. "We would wind up picking out your clothes, anyway."

"Remember, we don't have a ton of money." That was one thing that was stressing me out. "Go easy."

"Girl, we've got you covered." Lillith waved my words away like they weren't even an issue. "We've been around for so long that we have enough money to share."

I wanted to say no, but I couldn't. "We will pay you back."

"It's not expected." She winked at me.

Egan walked over and opened the door for me. "Let's get moving."

It took thirty minutes of following their scents to find them. We were four miles away from the mansion and in the thick of the woods.

"Hey, you." Donovan headed to me and lowered his lips to mine.

Even though he'd kissed and cuddled me last night, he hadn't kissed me lightheartedly, so it caught me off guard. "Hey."

"This is amazing." Axel's eyes were bright as he glanced around the place. "We could hear you coming the entire way."

"It's good that you're adjusting to your new senses."

This was something I'd planned to do, so I was proud that Roxy had gotten a head start. *Good job.*

She beamed with pride.

"Wolf hearing is one of your kind's strongest weapons," Egan explained. "Along with your nose."

"Speaking of which, you smell like fire." Donovan glanced at him. "I'm assuming you're not a wolf. What are you?"

"A dragon."

"Holy shit!" Axel exclaimed. "Those are real? Are witches, angels, and demons too?"

"Witches are, but none of the rest." Roxy chuckled. "Fae get mislabeled as witches and angels most of the time, and people get confused with vampires and demons since the vampires who've lost their humanity act without morals. However, witches can only use elemental magic with a sacrifice of sorts, usually blood if not more. Fae don't need that."

"Wow, that's crazy." Axel shuddered. "That vamp who attacked me was cold. I could see that."

Something shifted inside me, and the dizziness I'd felt around the teal-haired fae girl in the bathroom several weeks back slammed hard throughout me.

"Sadie." Donovan's voice cracked with concern. "Are you okay?"

"I ..." But my dizziness increased until I almost wobbled on my feet. "I don't know."

"What's wrong?" Donovan grabbed my shoulders, holding me in place. "Are you sick?"

"No ... dizzy." Granted, my stomach was rolling. Even though I couldn't hear or smell anything, I knew something was charging at us. "We need to go back. Now."

Egan tensed. "Let's go." He pointed at me. "Can you pick her up or do I need to?"

"I've got her." Donovan bent down and threw me over his shoulders.

Vomit inched up my throat. "I ..."

Realization sunk through me. We were no longer alone.

CHAPTER FIVE

"Let me down," I groaned. I didn't want to stand but having Donovan's shoulder rammed into my stomach was infinitely worse.

My head still swam, but I had to power through it. Something ... someone ... was almost here.

"You can barely stand." Donovan stopped in his tracks. "I don't know if it's smart."

"Something's here." This would hurt like a bitch. I rolled, desperate to get out of his grasp so I could face the incoming threat. I braced myself to hit the ground, but Donovan tightened his hold on my waist.

"Just give me a second," he said with annoyance. He grabbed my waist and set me down.

I managed to stay standing ... barely. "We aren't alone."

"What do you mean?" Egan tensed, and he circled us, scanning the area. "I don't ..."

Roxy came to my side and touched my arm. "Sadie, there isn't anything around us."

"No, she's right." Egan took in a deep breath. "We won't be alone much longer."

"If this is a joke because we left you two behind, it's not funny." Roxy glanced over her shoulder. "We've learned our lesson."

Axel glared at Egan and me as he stood protectively on her other side. "You two are scaring her, so stop it."

"No, I don't give a shit that you took them out here." The more they got in tune with nature, the better. "This isn't about you. There's ..." Two hauntingly gorgeous men stepped from between the trees.

The tallest one was a few inches shorter than Roxy, about my height. He had short royal blue hair and matching eyes. His golden skin glistened even in the shade of the trees.

The shorter one took a step toward us. His bright yellow hair hit the middle of this back, and his eyes were a light yellow. They looked eerie, especially against his pale skin, and they were locked on me. "What are you?"

"I think the better question is: Who are you?" Egan stepped in front of our group, protecting us.

"We aren't interested in you," the yellow-haired one spat as he focused on me. "It's her."

My brain felt like it had sunk to the bottom of a river. A strong current rushed inside my head, muddling my thoughts. "You think I should be forthcoming when I have no clue who you are?" I forced my legs forward, and by the grace of God, I didn't fall to my knees.

"We came here in peace, this one time." The blue-haired man lifted his chin. "It's wise not to anger us."

"What are these people?" Axel scratched the back of his neck. "By guy standards, these two are shorter than average."

"Do you find yourself funny?" the yellow-haired one said threateningly and glowered at Axel as my head swam harder. "Like we haven't heard that joke from your kind before."

Roxy snickered before she could tamp it down.

I hated to use the pack bond with them already, but it was necessary. *Do not make fun of them. These guys are fae.*

What the hell's going on? Axel sounded scared. *I'm hearing voices now.*

No, it's the pack bond. I didn't need them freaking out. *We can mind link when we want to say something between our group or individually.*

Fae? Donovan lifted an eyebrow. *I don't even know what that means.*

The fact that Donovan was staying on point was great. He'd accepted his wolf a little more, and he recognized the threat standing before us. I hoped the other things that came with being a wolf would be easier to accept after he'd had time to reflect on it.

Dude, remember Tinker Bell from Peter Pan? Axel actually sounded excited, but then he trailed off. *She was freaking hot. Is she for real?*

You keep thinking about hot girls, and I'll cut your dick off in your sleep, Roxy growled.

Oh, dear God. *Tinker Bell was based on fae.* We had to focus before we lost track of everything.

How the hell was their magic affecting me that way? I needed to protect my pack. Besides, the fae wanted to focus on me. "I'm a wolf shifter."

"We'll give you one last chance to answer honestly," the yellow-haired one said with disgust. "You should know how hard this is for us as we aren't known for our patience."

They were the most quick-tempered supernaturals when they had to travel to this world. Their presence here scared me.

You know, I always thought yellow was a happy color until this guy, Roxy quipped through the bond.

I didn't bother responding—my focus needed to stay solely on them—but I agreed with her. He was the angriest of the two. I could feel the power radiating off him. "I don't have any other answer to give."

The sun faded away, and darkness engulfed us. The yellow-haired fae's face morphed into one of pure disgust. "Fine, we'll do it the hard way."

A fallen branch lifted into the air.

It then shot across the opening toward me.

Egan moved to help me, but the branch was moving too fast. It reminded me of the bullet the vampire had fired at me.

My eyes locked on the branch, and despite my foggy brain, something inside me warmed. The friction built within a second and blasted out of me. The branch fell to the ground.

The yellow-haired one huffed. "What the hell?"

"Don't worry." The blue-haired man threw his hands to the side, and something surrounded me. He lifted his hand, and I felt like something was squeezing me.

I took a ragged breath and tried to push whatever was inside me out, but it sputtered like it was losing steam.

"Sadie!" Donovan yelled and touched my arm. "What's wrong?"

"I ... I don't know." None of this made any damn sense.

Egan charged at the blue-haired guy. "Stop hurting her."

"You don't get to intervene," the yellow-haired one said and pointed a finger at Egan, flinging him backward like he was a stick. "This doesn't concern you."

Egan slammed into a tree trunk and grunted. "Like hell,

it doesn't."

Now! Donovan yelled through the pack link.

He and Axel raced toward the two fae, and the blue-haired one lowered his head and bent down. He hit the ground with his hands, and the earth cracked apart as if he were drilling a hole. The lines traveled directly to Donovan and Axel.

Shit, we needed help. *Roxy, howl.* We needed to alert the vampires.

Yeah, okay. She threw her head back and pushed her wolf forward enough for a howl to escape.

The blue-haired fae diverted his attention to her. "They're calling for backup." He closed his hand, and her voice cut off like she had a muzzle.

I'd never fought a fae before, but I'd been told they were super powerful. The only way to weaken them was to keep them in this dimension long enough. They could only replenish their powers in the fae realm, but these guys weren't at risk of losing too much power. It was like they had stepped straight out of their dimension.

Something had to give. I was so damn tired of feeling helpless. I let anger fill my body and fuel every part of my being. I wasn't sure what I was doing—even my wolf whimpered—but I had to do something, and this felt right.

I watched as Donovan and Axel collapsed, and Roxy's eyes widened in pain. Egan was still plastered to the tree. We were all helpless against the two fae men.

Static electricity broke in my chest and flooded my body. I didn't know what the hell was happening, but I couldn't let my pack or Egan get hurt.

Several loud howls echoed around us.

"What the hell?" The yellow-haired one frowned. "I thought they were the only four wolves here."

"So did I," the one with blue hair replied without taking his focus off us. "Go check it out."

The yellow-haired one vanished.

I'd heard they could teleport, but seeing it was something else.

Axel linked with us, fear evident in every word. *Did that guy just disappear?*

With the yellow-haired one gone, whatever was holding me back released. However, the raging inferno inside me prevented me from walking, and I could barely breathe.

The yellow-haired one appeared again and touched his friend. "There's a whole pack heading this way. We'll be greatly outnumbered."

The blue-haired one frowned and shook his head. "Then we must leave."

Paws pounded loudly as the pack ran toward us. I didn't know what to expect, but having another pack come here was probably a bad thing. I didn't want to get into a territory dispute with them. That wouldn't do us any good, and it was damn clear that their pack was a lot larger than ours.

"Let's take her with us." The yellow-haired guy stepped in my direction.

"Oh, hell no," Donovan growled. "You're not taking her anywhere."

Egan's shirt ripped off him as his wings took hold. He took to the air, ready to fight.

Donovan stood on shaky legs but rushed with Egan, ready to protect me.

"We don't have time for this. They're almost here. We need to leave now," The blue-haired one said as he touched his friend's shoulder. "Don't get too comfortable," he threatened as he and the yellow-haired man disappeared into thin air.

"Is everyone okay?" Whatever was flowing through me soothed, but I was still too sick to move. I had no clue what was going on with me, but the fae didn't like it.

"My leg hurts," Axel complained as he limped over to Roxy. "Did he hurt you?"

"Not really." Roxy smiled slightly. "I just couldn't speak, even in my mind, or move."

"If another pack is coming, we should get out of here." Donovan took my hand and brushed his hand against my cheek. "Aren't packs territorial?"

"Yes." Egan landed back on the ground and retracted his wings into his back. "But leaving won't do us any good."

"Why?" Axel glanced toward the pack.

"Because they can smell and hear us." I glanced at Roxy. *Keep them behind me. They don't know how this works yet.*

Got it. Roxy nodded.

"If you can hear them, they can hear us. It goes both ways," I explained.

"What do we do?" Donovan asked, stepping firmly beside me.

You let me talk to them. If the pack realized we'd changed them, we'd have bigger problems. The pack also couldn't find out who I was. If they even got a hint that Tyler was my father, they'd hand us over in a heartbeat. Most packs did whatever they could to get on my father's good side.

But ... he started as Roxy came over and took his arm.

You have to let her do this. She glared at Donovan and then at Axel. *If they know how clueless you are, it'll be a red flag that something is off.*

Mostly, wolf shifters were scared. Turned wolves could

be mentally unstable or worse. There were so many horror stories about it.

Luckily, whatever had controlled me flowed out of my body and into the ground. I almost sighed with relief, but we were still in danger.

Ten wolves broke through the trees and stopped when they found the five of us. They sniffed the air but stayed where the fae had been.

It shocked me that they weren't growling at us. I'd expected an attack, although they were staring at us with distrust and wariness.

"We aren't here to harm you." They had to know that. I didn't want them to think we were here to take over their land.

"We know that." The deep voice came from behind a tree, and a man who was the same height as Donovan stepped into view. "Cassius called to inform us of his visitors."

The vampires did have our backs. That comforted me. Even though I trusted Katherine and Lillith, we weren't always like our parents. Look at me, for example. "Good. We got here last night and were just going for a walk to get a lay of the land."

"I'm Titan." The man had short brown hair and a full goatee. He was muscular like Donovan, and alpha power radiated off him. "The alpha of the pack."

"I'm ... Sadie." If I'd given them another name, they'd know I was lying. "Alpha of my pack." I had to stay strong, and hopefully, me being an alpha would throw off any suspicions that Tyler was my father.

Alpha? Donovan asked, his words full of concern. *Isn't your dad alpha?*

No, we had to start a new pack. All these semantics.

Otherwise, he could find us.

"A girl alpha ..." Titan lifted an eyebrow. "In the company of a dragon and recently attacked by fae." His forest green eyes locked on Egan. "You guys are far more interesting than Cassius indicated."

Okay .... maybe they weren't on our side after all. "I'm not sure what you're getting at."

"I need to know what's going on." Titan crossed his arms and examined each one of us. "Your presence puts us in danger due to our close proximity to the vampire mansion. I may be a nice guy, but I can't risk the safety of my pack."

"I don't know why the fae are after us." That was the God's honest truth. Unless my father had done something to piss them off... but I wasn't willing to divulge who my father was yet, even though he probably already knew.

He tilted his head and narrowed his eyes. "Don't worry. There might be a way to find answers."

"Please, enlighten us," Donovan said protectively.

"You're coming with us." Titan's jaw ticked, ready for us to argue.

That didn't sound good, but we were at a clear disadvantage. Only ten wolves stood directly behind him in our view, but at least twenty were still hidden in the woods. Even with Egan on our side, there was no way we could get out of this. We were completely outnumbered. "And if we go willingly, do you promise that none of us will be injured?"

"Of course." He met my eyes and nodded. "You can come willingly, or we'll force you. The option is yours."

There wasn't the stench of a lie, so I nodded. However, there was always a loophole. I just hoped we weren't walking into a situation blind.

CHAPTER SIX

R oxy linked only to me. *Are you sure this is wise? Alphas aren't the most tolerant.*

It was easy to know how many wolves were in a conversation. You could sense the consciousness of each person involved. *Some say there are a few out there.* I'd never met any before, but there had to be a first time, surely.

Her shoulders dropped. *Let's hope you're not wrong.*

Me too.

I opened the pack link to everyone. *Roxy and Axel, stay in the back and keep an eye out. Donovan and I will stay in front.* In times like these, I wished Egan could be part of the pack, but he had his own pack to take care of—if dragons were even called that.

Despite not having a link, Egan stayed behind, putting Roxy between him and Axel. He knew she was the weakest one here even with the two newly turned shifters. Though they'd never shifted to their wolves, their power was visible.

"No funny business," Titan warned. "It's as much of a risk for us to take you to our pack as it is for you to go. So, a little bit of trust will be required on both sides."

"More on ours than yours." Egan cleared his throat and pointed at his bare chest. "Do you mind if I run back and get a shirt?"

"Are you modest?" Titan chuckled.

Usually, shifters didn't think twice about nudity, especially shirtless men, but it would give Egan the opportunity to alert the vampires of what was going on. I hadn't even considered trying to get one of us to do it. There was so much I needed to learn to become a great leader.

Egan kept a straight face. "No, but a shirtless dragon waltzing in might add more to the buzz."

Titan's face tensed like he wasn't thrilled. "Okay, you aren't needed, really. The fae were focused on her." He pointed at me and waved his hand, dismissing Egan. "Only these four are required. We should get acquainted since we'll be spending time around each other for a little while."

"Well, I'll go change and find you." Egan stared the alpha down. "It'd be good for your pack to meet me as well. I'll be there as long as those four are."

It amazed me how much of a true friend Egan had turned out to be. There was no doubt in my mind he had our backs.

"Fine." Titan lifted a hand. "You can follow our scents, right?"

"Yeah, I can." Egan glanced at me before turning toward the house. "I won't be long."

Our group watched Egan head back toward the vampire house, and soon, he was out of sight.

I linked with the other three. *Even though they seem good-intentioned, don't let your guard down.* Maybe the alpha planned to surprise us even though it would be difficult.

"All right, let's get moving." Titan walked past his wolves, heading straight down the middle.

The four of us fell into step behind him, and the rest of the wolves took up the rear. A few sniffed, taking in our scents, but none came off as threatening.

The woods were brimming with animals, more so now than they'd been at night. Scents of deer, rabbits, foxes, and so many others intermingled in the air. Even the woods back home didn't have as much wildlife as here. "How big is your pack?" It couldn't be as large as I'd initially expected.

"My pack sits at one hundred and three." Titan spouted the number off like I'd asked him his name. "Why do you ask?"

"Wow, really?" Then they had to eat something beyond the animals in the woods. "The woods are thriving."

"Ah ... yes." He grinned proudly. "That's because we only take what's absolutely necessary and nothing more. We don't kill for fun."

That was something Dad and his cronies regularly did. They enjoyed hunting and didn't mind wasting. "That's noble."

"How big is your pack?" Titan asked as he walked lazily like he didn't have a care in the world.

I didn't want to tell him, but it wasn't like I could refuse. I'd just asked him the same question. "We have four."

"Four?" That made him stop mid-step and glance at us. "This is your entire pack?"

"Yeah, so what?" Roxy crossed her arms, sticking up for me. "We might be small, but we're mighty."

Is that a big deal? Donovan took my hand.

Kind of. I didn't want to lie to them. *It means he knows we're a new pack.*

Axel stood close to Roxy, on high alert. *Is a new pack such a bad thing?*

It usually means we left a pack. Which could come off as suspicious, especially since fae were chasing after us. *Which is not normal.*

Whatever you do, do not tell them that you were bitten, Roxy added.

Can't they tell? Donovan glanced over his shoulder at the twenty wolves following close behind.

No. The fact that Roxy hadn't alerted me to anything odd with them this morning comforted me. *You don't have any disabilities.*

Why does that matter? Axel asked.

Most people who are bitten don't survive the change, and the ones who do usually have a deformity. It was a blessing that they didn't have one.

How is that possible? Donovan sounded confused and slightly concerned. *Does that mean something is wrong?*

I suspect it's because you were both already part wolf. That was what I had banked on the night we'd turned them. *You already had an animal as part of you. All we did was allow them more control over your body. The ones who have problems are those who didn't have an animal within them, to begin with. It changes their core senses and can't convert it all in the time of the shift.*

That actually makes sense, Roxy replied. *I hadn't thought of it like that.*

"How long have you four been a pack?" Titan asked, interrupting our internal conversation.

"For a short while." I didn't want to answer that question directly. The more we revealed about how new we were, the more suspicious he'd be.

A clearing appeared in front of us, and I could already see several small cabins.

We were getting close to Titan's pack.

He stopped in front of us and turned. "I'm taking you into my pack. The least you can do is answer my questions."

"I'm not sure why it's relevant." I refused to be bullied by anyone any longer. I'd finally stood up to my father; it seemed asinine to stop holding my own now.

"Because I'm vouching for you." Titan glared at me and clenched his hands. "By allowing you to meet my pack, I'm introducing your pack's problems into mine, and I'd like to know what the hell is going on."

Donovan lifted his chin. "We didn't ask for your help."

"Oh, I'm sorry." Sarcasm laced Titan's words. "Someone didn't howl for help?"

"It was meant for the vampires." I should've realized that was why they'd come. "Not you."

"Nonetheless, we came and helped." Titan's nostrils flared with clear annoyance. "And by doing so, the fae are aware of us, which means they've lumped us in with you."

A wolf behind us growled, unhappy with our uncooperativeness.

"So, what?" Hopefully, Egan would be there soon. We were getting in over our heads. "You're going to attack us now?"

Titan's shoulders straightened, and he faced me head-on. "Should we?"

A woman stepped from the clearing into view. "What's going on out here?" She had shoulder-length blonde hair, was about my height, and had eyes that matched mine.

"I told you to stay back at the house until we got more information from them." Titan tensed even more but didn't face her. Instead, he stepped in front of me as if to block the woman from my view.

"And you know how well I like to listen." She didn't break stride as her voice came closer and became clearer.

"Winter, please go back." The alpha closed his eyes as if he knew she wouldn't listen.

"As your mate, I get to assist in pack affairs." She tsked as she reached his side. When her gaze landed on mine, her eyes widened, and she stumbled as if she'd seen a ghost.

But I'd never seen this lady in my entire life, which meant she must know who I was. Once again, Daddy Dearest was a huge pain in my ass. There went any chance of working together.

Titan caught her and scowled at me. "What the hell did you just do?"

"Nothing." This lady could easily pit her mate against me. It would only take one word through the pack link. *Guys, get ready to run.*

Axel linked as he stepped behind Roxy, ready to protect her. *You realize there's no way in hell we can get out of here.*

We have to try. Donovan sounded focused. *They might not expect a direct attack.*

"Like hell—" Titan growled.

"No, she didn't." Winter pushed him out of her way and rubbed her eyes. "It can't be ..."

A few wolves appeared beside us, baring their teeth.

Great, this was going so well. "Look, I didn't do anything to her."

"Leave her alone." Winter walked over to me, shooing the wolves away. "All of you, go back to the pack. We will be back there shortly."

"Now—" Titan started, but Winter turned her icy stare on him.

"Do you need to go with them?" She spread her feet shoulder-width apart, ready for a battle.

"Dammit." Titan frowned and looked at the twenty-nine wolves standing there, unsure what to do. "You heard her. Go."

All of them took off without a moment's hesitation, except for one. He hung back and whined for a second.

"It's fine," Titan reassured them. "Go ahead."

A vein in Donovan's neck bulged as he watched the strange woman. "I won't let you hurt her."

"I would never." Her musky lavender scent filled my nose, and it smelled familiar. Her blue eyes took me in. "Sadie, is that really you?"

There it was. It confirmed my worst fear. Dad would be here within the hour. "Who are you?"

"Oh, God. It really is you." Her hands shook as she reached for me but stopped. Tears spilled down her cheeks. "How is this possible?"

"Baby, you're scaring me." Titan stood next to her, and all his anger melted away and was replaced with concern. "Sadie is dead. You told me that."

They thought I was dead? How did that make any sense?

"That's what the bastard told me." She wiped the moisture from under her eyes, and throwing caution to the wind, she wrapped her arms around me. "But that rose-gold hair and the vanilla scent—it has to be you."

I tensed, unsure what the hell to do. "Uh ... who are you?" I didn't push her off me because the hug was oddly comforting. It felt like I should know her, like she was a missing piece of my soul.

"Winter ..." Titan touched her arm to get her attention. "This could be a trick. If it's her—"

"Shut it," Winter hissed and pulled back slightly. "I'm having a moment with my daughter."

I'd hoped they'd be a decent pack willing to help us. It had been a long shot, but not every shifter or supernatural was thrilled with my father. But for her to try to mind fuck me was not okay.

I stepped out of her hold, and pure hatred filled me. She didn't smell of a lie, but the fae could be involved in some way. Hate felt better than confusion. What kind of sicko would play with someone's emotions like this? "Do you think this is funny?"

Why is this woman claiming to be your mother? Donovan's confusion hit me. *That sounds like a pretty stupid thing to do.*

Because I never met her. My wolf howled inside me, and electricity grew under my skin. *She died giving birth to me.*

"There's no way in hell you're her mother." Roxy marched to my other side. "Unless you were raised from the dead."

"Is that what he told you?" Winter scoffed and ran her fingers through her hair. "He told you I died?"

"What other explanation is there?" Of course, now it all made sense. "Unless you ran off, not wanting to raise me."

"That's not it at all." Her mouth dropped open, and she stumbled back. "I guess I get why it appears that way."

"Appears that way?" Oh, no. She didn't get to play the victim. If this was true, not only had my mother left me behind, but she'd left me with a prick of a father who'd treated me worse than dirt. "If you really are her, then you're a sorry excuse for a mother."

"You don't get to talk to my mate that way!" Titan bellowed, his wolf coming to the forefront.

"Calm down," Winter snarled at him. "I get you're protecting me, but you need to butt out."

"Winter—"

"No." She jabbed her finger at him. "This is between me and my ... *daughter*." The word broke at the end.

Hope filled me, and that was a dangerous game. I had to squash it before my heart got broken.

"Tyler caught me that night," she started and focused on the trees behind me. "It was a week after your birth. He was so livid that you were a girl, despite us knowing the whole time, and threatened to kill you. He'd thought he could wish a boy."

Now that sounded like Dad.

"He was yelling and screaming at me and you the entire time." Winter cringed as the memory replayed in her mind. "He was supposed to be out of town. Hell, I saw him drive away. I had it all planned. We were going to stay with some distant relatives here in the Smoky Mountains."

"Still not understanding the leaving her behind part," Roxy snapped.

"Will you give her a damn minute?" Titan spat back.

Roxy, chill. I needed to hear this out. *Please.*

Fine, she grumbled.

"I'm sorry," I said and shot Roxy a look of warning. "Please continue."

"When I got to the nursery, you weren't there." Winter placed a hand on her chest, and her eyes filled with pain. "The head maid stepped through the door and informed me that Tyler had carried you away with him to bury, and he would be back shortly. She must have believed it because she didn't smell of a lie. Her words hit me so hard that I didn't question it. Not after his threats. All I knew was that I hadn't been able to protect you. That was when I became resolved to run. I had to get away before he returned because I couldn't live with him or the memory of you."

"And he told me you had died." He'd kept the story the same so it would be easy to keep track of. He was smart like that. "I got left behind with a dad who didn't even want me. He just didn't want you to have me."

"Yes, you did." She licked her lips.

"But he never smelled of a lie." But she didn't either at this moment. That couldn't be possible. One of them had to be lying."

"You've got to understand." Winter lifted a shaky hand. "As a child, Tyler was trained to be able to lie without his scent giving it away. He gloated to me about that fact several times while I was pregnant with you. He said the trick was believing the lie but that only a select few can actually accomplish it."

That made sense, even though I'd never heard it was possible before. "But that's insane."

"It is." She pulled at her ponytail. "But there is so much more to the story."

"Oh, really?" I wasn't sure there could be more. There was no way she could top this.

"Because he isn't your biological father."

CHAPTER SEVEN

"**O**kay, that's enough." Donovan pulled me behind him and stared Winter down. "I've let you say more than I wanted to, but you've gone too far."

"Hey ..." Titan stalked over to Donovan and got in his face. "Don't even pretend you're not okay with this. My mate thinks she's seeing her dead daughter. If anything, the fae may be fucking with us."

"You two need to calm your asses down." Winter squeezed between the two men and shoved them apart. "She is my daughter, and why are you bringing fae into this?"

"Because two fae men just attacked us," Axel said. "Apparently, you all heard our call for help."

"What? Fae?" Winter shook her head and focused on me. "Has anything weird happened lately?"

"Weird?" What was she digging for? I wouldn't bare my heart and soul to her if that was what she expected.

Roxy rolled her eyes. "If you'd call her disappearing and reappearing several feet away and stopping bullets strange, I'd say yes."

"No." Winter's shoulders sagged. "This isn't good."

"Do you mind explaining, or are you going to keep babbling and making no sense?" If she knew something useful, now would be the time.

"It's your father." She blew out a breath.

"Are you saying Titan's my dad?" There was no way it could be him. If he thought I was his child, he wouldn't be standing there so stoically, would he? Maybe she had terrible taste in men. If her story was true, she had chosen Tyler first.

"What?" Mom jerked her head at Titan and back at me. "Oh, no. He's not your father."

Tyler wasn't my father and neither was Titan. There was a third man in this mix. And here I thought once you found your mate, you were locked for life. Was she really saying that everything I knew was wrong? For whatever reason, I found this hilarious and began to laugh.

Sadie, are you okay? Roxy asked as she came closer from one side and Axel walked over to the other.

They were surrounding me, which turned my laughter into an ugly cry. Nothing made sense. I'd supposedly found my dead mom and learned that the man I'd grown up with wasn't my father. This had to be a dream. Hell, maybe a nightmare. *Peachy. I'm just peachy.*

Peachy? Axel cut his eyes at me. *Really?*

Yeah, maybe that hadn't been the best word, which made me laugh even harder. I was teetering between losing my mind and keeping my sanity.

Winter reached around Donovan and touched my hand. "Honey, I know it's a lot to take in."

"No." I jerked away from her and glared. "You don't get to drop a bombshell like that on me. You don't have the right to act concerned." Hell, it probably was all an act. "This is a lot more than that. You're telling me that Tyler isn't my father, but he raised me. Not you ... him." He'd killed every other child after me. Why hadn't he done the same to me? "I find it hard to believe. You have to be lying." Maybe she was delusional and believed it—if the fae weren't involved.

"What?" She stilled and rubbed her arms. "No, I'm not."

"He would've killed me if this is all true." Did she think I was that gullible or stupid? "So, spare me this act." *Let's go.* I couldn't stay here and listen to this anymore.

I'd been around my dad long enough to learn that good manipulators seemed sincere.

Gladly. Donovan took my hand and stepped beside me as Roxy moved to his side.

"No, please don't go." Winter had figured out we were leaving. "There's so much I'd like to know about you."

My hesitation said it all. The fact that I wanted to stay told me that I believed her. "I'm sorry. I can't." The longer I stayed, the worse I'd hurt.

Winter pivoted to her mate. "Titan, do something. She can't leave."

"Honey, they aren't our pack members." Titan sighed and touched her shoulder. "I can't make them do anything unless we force them."

His suggestion didn't sit well with me. *We'd better hurry.*

Neither one had spoken, but I heard people heading our way. We weren't getting away without a fight. It figured. I should've expected it from someone like her.

The faint scent of brimstone hit my nose, and I almost cried in relief. Egan would be here soon, and he might give them pause. He could light their homes on fire within seconds if needed.

"You don't want to do this." I steadied myself, needing to appear strong even if I was a quivering mess inside. "We have reinforcements coming."

Winter sniffed the air. "What is that?"

"A dragon." Titan lowered his head. "They have aligned with a dragon shifter."

"I'd recommend telling your pack to back off." If she wanted to pretend to be a good mother, this wasn't the way. "Forcing me to stay is no better than what you're accusing my father of."

She inhaled sharply right as Egan stepped through the tree line and came into view.

As soon as he took in our rigid stances, he rushed over. "What's going on?"

"Apparently, Sadie's mom is back from the dead." Roxy bared her teeth at Winter. "And she's decided to force Sadie to stay here."

Egan stuck his huge chest out, reminding me of a brick wall. "That's not happening."

"You're right." Winter gazed at the ground, appearing regretful. "I can't make her stay here, no matter how much I want to."

"Good." I spun on my heel and marched to the woods, ready to get back to the vampires. My pack and Egan followed behind me, blocking me from Winter's view.

"Sadie?" Winter's voice cracked. "Please, I just want to tell you everything."

"I think you've said enough." I needed time to process what she'd said before I considered hearing more. Maybe if she hadn't told me Tyler wasn't my father, things would have been different. Probably not, but that didn't matter.

"But—"

"Leave her alone," Titan said gently. "She needs space,

and I think you do too before you do something you'll regret."

The sound of the wolves heading in our direction stopped. Titan must have called them off, thankfully. I had a feeling it had more to do with Egan showing up than anything else.

"She's alive ..." Winter whispered, and a slight sob reached my ears.

Roxy used our pack bond to link. *Do you think she's telling the truth? She didn't reek of a lie, and her heart rate didn't increase.*

It doesn't matter, Donovan growled. *If Sadie doesn't want to stay, then we're getting out of here.*

Hey, you can't just waltz in here and trump me, Roxy admonished. *I've been her best friend since kindergarten.*

And I'm her mate, Donovan said naturally. *I will always trump you.*

The two of them were making me feel loved, which I was pretty sure was the point, but my heart sped up at the way Donovan had called himself my mate like he'd accepted our bond. Maybe with him firmly by my side, I could find some peace and happiness before Dad found me and killed me.

Winter's words replayed in my mind. "He's not your father." That was impossible. And if not him or Titan, then who? That was what she wanted me to come back for, but I refused.

Aw, hell no, Roxy challenged. *You weren't there the day she pissed her pants at school and I covered for her while she changed.*

Axel snickered and stepped between her and me.

Are you serious? I couldn't believe that bitch. *You're giving up childhood secrets about me?*

Oh, please. Roxy grinned. *You forgot all about the other stuff for a second. I deserve a medal.*

Her logic astonished me at times. *This is how you justify it?*

You'll get me back. She winked at me. *I'm sure.*

Damn straight, I will. Honestly, I probably wouldn't. She'd had my back that day, even at the expense of the other wolves tormenting her more than usual. Most shifters gave her the same amount of respect as my Dad did to her family: none. The little bit she had was when I was around because they didn't want to piss off the alpha's daughter. They believed I had influence over my dad.

That was how charming he came off ... until he wasn't and people wound up a bloody mess or dead with a bullet between their eyes.

"So ... why would that woman lie about being your mother?" Egan asked when we were a safe distance away.

"I'm not sure she did." I hated to admit it out loud, but it was true. "She didn't smell of a lie, but maybe the fae met with them beforehand to see if they could trick me into telling her something."

"I doubt that." Egan scratched the back of his neck. "Fae don't like to work with anyone outside their race. And let's be real; most never leave the fae realm."

Axel scanned the area for threats. "Why is that?"

Egan dropped his hands by his sides. "Because the longer they're here in our dimension, the more their power weakens. Their magic is tied directly to their realm."

The only real threat that hung over my father was the fae. They were the strongest, even more so than the dragons. But everyone knew that once a fae stayed here too long, they could be beaten. Dad didn't worry about the dragons since there were so few of them. He had numbers on his side, including some outside the wolf shifter race. He'd been building up favors and attacking the smaller packs, nests, and whatever else that wouldn't cause an issue.

He was a real dictator, and no one but a few realized the depth of his influence and hate.

Donovan squeezed my hand gently. "So, a different dimension. That sounds like a movie."

"Yeah, it does, but it's real." I knew enough information about the fae to be dangerous, but that was it. Egan seemed to have more knowledge about them. "Most fae can teleport, and the few who can't use portals around the world."

"If they're so strong, you'd think they'd find a way over here." Donovan pursed his lips. "Like find a way to bind them to our land or crossbreed with the supernaturals here."

"Fae prefer their world." A smile spread across Egan's face. "There's no pollution. The sky is a beautiful blue-green. The climate is perfect within the middle region, and there's a sense of peace that will never be found here."

Those details were super intricate. "It's like you've been there."

When Egan didn't respond, Roxy jerked her head toward him. "Shut up. There's no way."

"A long time ago, my kind came from Fae." He shrugged. "When a dragon turns of age, they can go on a pilgrimage to see where we were born. But I've only heard stories since I've never been to the Fae realm."

"And they allow you in there?" That surprised me. Fae didn't like people on their land.

"Because we came from there, they allow our kind one visit in our lifetime." Egan seemed whimsical. "But to answer your question, fae are strictly forbidden to date outside their race. They're elitists in the truest sense, not because they hate other races but because they don't want to become tied to this heathen Earth."

"Heathen Earth?" That sounded like it had come from him and not fae.

"I don't completely disagree with them." Egan lifted a brow, not even trying to lie.

"Hey, I hear you." Roxy pointed at him. "Earth sucks ass most of the time."

The mansion came into view, and I spotted Katherine and Lillith sitting on patio furniture around a firepit. When they saw us approaching, Lillith stood and rushed to us.

"We've been worried about you but didn't want to interfere with the pack introductions." Lillith pulled me into a hug. "Egan told us everything. Are you okay?"

Her sweet scent comforted me. "Yeah, I'm fine."

"Uh ... what am I?" Roxy waved a hand in front of herself. "Chopped liver?"

"No, but they didn't seem nearly as interested in you as her." Lillith didn't look at her, her focus on me. "What can we do?"

Great, I hated being the center of attention. In fact, I'd rather be ignored. "Nothing." I forced myself to yawn, needing to get away. "I'm actually really tired."

I could feel the displeasure radiating off Roxy, but she kept her mouth shut. She knew I retreated when I felt overwhelmed.

"Oh, you woke up about two hours ago," Lillith pushed but apparently decided to drop it. "But I guess you've been through an ordeal."

Roxy mumbled, "You don't know the half of it."

Not helping. I glared at her, wanting her to shut it down. I had a feeling as soon as I escaped to the comfort of my room, she'd tell them everything. Better her than me.

"Why don't you go take a nap, and the rest of us can run into town and grab some necessities and clothes." Egan was a good friend. "I'm sure Roxy and Lillith have you covered."

Sweet baby Jesus. That sounded excellent. I could hide in my room and not have to deal with the adventure of clothes shopping with those two. "If they're willing, that sounds perfect."

If I didn't know how much you'd complain, I wouldn't allow it, Roxy teased. *But I shall let it pass.* "Hell yeah. Let's go. I'm ready to get out of these sweatpants."

"Axel, do you mind shopping for me?" Donovan moved closer to my side. "I'm going to stay behind with her."

"Fine." Axel frowned. "But you better remember what I'm doing for you."

"Oh, please." Katherine stood and strolled over to us. "Roxy is your mate. You wouldn't want it any other way."

"Come on." Lillith pulled the keys from her pocket. "I've been ready to go for a while."

I hurried up the stairs before they could change their minds. "All of you have fun." I walked through the door with Donovan following on my heels.

None of the vampires were in the kitchen, and some of the tension left me. I wasn't in the mood to talk. I breezed through the room and headed straight to the stairs, bypassing the living room.

Damn, it'd only been one night, but it felt much longer. So much had happened, and it hadn't even been twenty-four hours.

I hurried up the stairs, ready to hide. I opened the door to our room and almost crumbled. I'd been afraid that I'd have to pretend to be okay a little longer.

"Hey," Donovan whispered huskily as he pulled me into his arms. "It's okay to be upset."

That was the first time anyone had ever said anything like that to me. It had been drilled into me that showing my emotions and letting them rule me would make me weak. To have someone comforting me felt foreign.

I rested my head on his chest, and I whispered the words that scared me to even think. "What if she's my mother? What if I threw away the one chance I had to get answers? What if I'd ruined it all?"

CHAPTER EIGHT

"If she's really your mother and cares, then you haven't ruined a damn thing," Donovan said as he stared into my eyes. "And if she cuts you off after dumping all that on you at once, she doesn't deserve to know you."

"I just don't understand." The hurt bubbled to the surface now that I didn't have to pretend to be strong. I only hoped Donovan wasn't disappointed by it. "She ran off without even trying to check." If I'd been in her place, knowing that Tyler could lie, I'd have demanded to see the body or gone to the grave.

"Neither do I." He cupped my face and lowered his forehead to mine. "But it doesn't matter. You have people who love you all around you."

I hated to be that girl, but I couldn't help it. "Yes, and a dad who tried to force me into doing whatever he wanted and is now hunting us."

"Maybe that's true, but..." He took my hand and placed it on his chest. "First off, Roxy loves you completely. That girl would go to the ends of the earth for you."

She had been the one constant in my life. "Without her,

I'm not sure how I would've turned out." In the moments when Dad had almost broken me, she'd kept me pieced together. Despite my dad insisting she was weak, her friendship and support were the only things that had kept me strong.

"And you have Katherine, Lillith, and Egan who care." His free arm wrapped around my waist. "Those three left school to stand by you."

Even though I realized they'd saved us, their total sacrifice hadn't sunk in until now. "You're right." Now I felt worse. Anyone who got close to me wound up with a target on their back.

"And there's me," he murmured.

Some of the pain receded, and my heart rate increased. "I know you care."

"You know it's more than that." His eyes darkened to navy as a smirk crossed his face. "But you're going to make me say it, aren't you?"

"I'd never make you say anything you didn't want to." He had to believe me. I refused to be like my father.

"Which makes me love you even more."

My breath caught, and my heart fluttered. "Don't say it before you're ready."

"I knew it the moment I saw you." He chuckled, and his lips lowered closer to mine. "All those years of keeping everyone at arm's length, and you tore my walls down with a glance."

"That's not the feeling I got." He had been combative with me. Hell, I'd been the same way. Being drawn to a human hadn't been ideal. It had taken a while for me to realize there was a faint wolf inside him.

"Well, I was pissed." He pulled me closer so our waists touched. "And scared. But you fought it yourself."

"To protect you." It hadn't done us any good, though. My dad and Brock had gotten the vampire to attack him and his friend when I wouldn't obey his order to date the alpha heir of the second-largest pack.

"You sure seem to do that a lot." He kissed my lips gently, and our bond opened to each other. "As long as I'm with you, I'll be okay. I love you, Sadie."

"I love you too." I didn't want to miss the opportunity to say it back. Every day, I grew older, and tomorrow seemed more uncertain than yesterday. "And I'm sorry I turned you. It was selfish. I couldn't bear the thought of losing you."

"It was shocking at first, but you made the right choice." He deepened our kiss. *I'd have done the same thing for you.*

He lifted me, and I wrapped my legs around his waist. I could already feel his hardness through our jeans. He stalked across the room and laid me on the bed. He leaned over me, his breath hitting my face.

I closed my eyes, enjoying his touch. This was something I would always crave ... would always need.

His hand slipped inside my shirt and under my bra, teasing my breast. His touch nearly drove me wild.

"Oh, God," I moaned, ready for him.

"Are you sure you're okay with this?" He stilled, concern etched into his face. "I don't want to take advantage of you after what you just went through."

"Please take advantage," I almost whimpered. *I need you.* I'd been craving more of him since two nights ago. Only a couple of days had passed since our first time, but so much had changed that it felt like weeks if not more.

Any hesitancy left his face, and his mouth crashed onto mine. *I'm so glad you said that.* His fingers pinched my nipples, kindling the fire inside me.

Need overwhelmed me, and my fingers trembled as

they unfastened his jeans. I slipped my hand inside his boxers, enjoying the feel of him. He was ready, and I was right there with him.

He lifted me off the bed, removed my shirt, and unfastened my bra, discarding them on the floor. His mouth replaced his hand on my breast, and his tongue flicked, making me dizzy.

Desperation took hold, and I pushed his jeans and boxers down, making it easier to stroke him as he worked on me.

Removing his mouth from my breast, he groaned, "God, that feels good." He lay on his side next to me, flicked open the buttons of my jeans, and yanked my pants and panties off my body. His hands slid between my legs and rubbed against me.

We quickened the pace on each other; our breathing turned ragged. My body tensed, but I wasn't ready for the release.

I removed his hands from me and crawled onto the bed on my knees. *Join me.*

He jumped to his feet, not needing to be asked twice. He grabbed my waist, about to pull me over, but I shook my head.

No, this way. I didn't want to be tempted to claim him. If I faced him, my wolf would go crazy, and he wasn't ready for that. It would intensify our bond and make his animal more volatile. He needed more time to acclimate before we stirred anything else up.

Well, okay then. He placed himself behind me and thrust inside.

He hit the deepest spot inside me right away, and I placed my hands down in front of me. When he slammed in a second time, I matched his pace, driving him deeper. I'd never had sex this way before, thinking it was too animalistic, but it was more sensual than I'd ever imagined.

His fingers dug into my sides, driving me closer to the edge.

Sadie, I want to claim you, he growled, not slowing down. *I want all of you.*

You'll have me after you shift at least once. It was so damn hard to form a complete thought as his hand snuck around my waist and touched my most sensitive spot. *It'll be easier that way, but I'm all yours. I love you.*

He rubbed in circles as his body tensed, slamming into me over and over again. *Damn right you are.* His body shook as he orgasmed, causing my own to rock through me. He growled deep in my ear, *I love you too.* We collapsed onto the bed.

THE NEXT WEEK or so passed in a blur. Each day, Roxy, Egan, Axel, Donovan, and I would go out into the woods to let them acclimate their animals to nature. They'd both tried shifting the past few days and hadn't accomplished it yet, but they were getting closer.

It was strange, but in a way, their wolves were like newborns. They had always been there, but their presence hadn't been strong. Even shifters didn't fully transition to their wolves until they were teenagers.

"All right, let's try this again." Axel finished off his plate of pancakes. "I'm going to turn all wolfy today."

"I'm sure you'll manage, dear." Julie grinned as she washed off the griddle she'd used to cook breakfast. She'd been cooking our group breakfast every morning.

"How I remember enjoying food like that." Athan

stared longingly at the food left on my and Roxy's plates. "Now it doesn't even smell good."

"At least, we don't have to worry about calories anymore," Katherine said, trying to put a silver lining on it. "We can drink as much blood as we want and not gain weight."

"Or lose it," Lillith grumbled. "Since I was vampire born, we gain weight until we reach our full height. Thankfully, I had a fast metabolism because, when you're younger, you don't consider that your body will soon be frozen for all eternity."

"Oh, please." Roxy waved her off and took a bite of her bacon. "You're skinny, and you know it."

Donovan took a sip of his coffee. "I'll tell you what. I thought I had an appetite before, but it was nothing like now."

"It's because your animal burns off calories too." Egan still had a plate full of food left after he'd eaten two. "Especially with how much we're going out into the woods. I haven't been this hungry since I grew scales."

"Well, as fun as this is." I stood and carried my plate to the sink. "We need to get moving. We don't need Dad showing up before we're prepared."

"We don't need your father showing up at all." Cassius strolled into the kitchen, twisting his wedding band around his finger. "Since we refrain from drinking too much blood, we aren't the strongest nest around. That's one reason we stay hidden."

"Even with being an original?" Donovan stood and grabbed his empty plate and Axel's. "I'm a little surprised."

"Yeah, vampires are meant to drink more blood than we do." Cassius walked to the fridge and pulled out a pouch of blood. "We drink enough to sustain ourselves and nothing more. The more gluttonous you become, the more vulnerable you are to turn dark. I enjoy standing out in the sunlight and doing things most other vampires can no longer do."

I couldn't argue with that logic.

"Are you going to hurry up or not?" Roxy winked at me and turned her head in Egan's direction. "We're ready to go, and once again, we're waiting on your ass."

Egan held his plate near his face and shoveled food into his mouth with his fork. He paused to chew.

The poor guy had been hurrying the entire time. He'd gotten here before us, but he ate three times the amount we did. Roxy gave him hell at every opportunity.

"Immm tryin'," he muttered and scooped another large bite into his mouth.

"Leave him alone." It wasn't like we had a ton of pressing things to do today.

Oh, let me have some fun. She pouted at me. *He's hard to rile up at times. He's always so kind and nice. Let me poke him when I can without feeling bad.*

Luther entered the room and cleared his throat. "Do you mind if I tag along?"

That was the most I'd heard him speak since we'd gotten here and started hanging around the vampires more often. We'd even played game night with them last night, and Donovan and I had kicked all their asses in poker.

"Sure," I said at the same time Julie said, "It's probably not a good idea."

I stopped short, not wanting to cause any familial problems.

"Oh, come on." Luther pointed at me. "She said I could go."

"Axel and Donovan are new wolves." Julie turned the

faucet off and dried her hands on a towel. "I'd hate for you to get injured if they shift."

"I can ..." Egan choked on his food. "... watch him."

I glared at Roxy. *See, you should feel bad. The poor guy is gonna die, rushing for you.*

Oh, he's not. Roxy scrunched her nose at me, but she couldn't hide the wave of guilt. *He's fine.*

"Luther's eyes widened with hope. "See, the dragon won't let anything happen to me."

"That dragon has a name," Julie scolded. "Are you sure it won't be a problem, *Egan?*" she asked, emphasizing the name as she narrowed her eyes at her son.

Egan took a sip of his water and shook his head. "It won't be a problem." His plate was empty, and Roxy snatched it from him and took it to the sink.

Babe, guilt is pouring off you. Axel snickered as he teased her. He picked up the bag with the extra change of clothes that we'd been taking with us.

You better think again before you say anything else. She held her head high and marched out the door, not bothering to glance back at us.

Donovan wrapped an arm around my waist and linked to Axel. *Your mate is a handful.*

Don't get all cocky. Axel headed to the door. *Your mate has pink hair, so don't think she doesn't have a temper.*

It's true. I kissed Donovan's cheek. *I do. You've been warned and should be scared.*

Maybe I want to make you mad. Donovan waggled his brows. *You might have to teach me a few lessons.*

"I don't even need to know what you're saying mentally to each other to feel the sexual tension in the air." Lillith lobbed a balled-up paper towel at us. "Go outside and get him shifting before you two get naked and make us all see things we'll never forget."

I closed my eyes, wishing that could make me invisible. "We weren't doing anything." I couldn't even lie that well.

"Yeah, whatever." Lillith wouldn't let it go, even with her dad in the room. "The beating of your hearts is loud, and the sweet scent of arousal is heavy."

"Okay, I'll see you all later." I ran to the door, feeling unable to get out of there fast enough.

I could hear Donovan's laughter from outside. "She's my mate. Don't even try to make us feel bad about it."

Without slowing, I headed straight to our usual spot, passing Roxy and Axel. The rest were behind me, laughing at my expense. I was okay with that because it gave me a few seconds to myself.

I was both surprised and disappointed that Winter hadn't come back around. It was a double-edged sword, and neither alternative was ideal. I wanted her to want to talk to me, but I also wanted her to respect me as I tried to figure out if there was any truth to her story.

My wolf told me it was true. None of the deception clues had been there, but it seemed so far-fetched.

I reached the small clearing and slowed, allowing my pack, Egan, and Luther to catch up.

Egan stayed at the edge like always, close enough to provide suggestions but far enough away to keep an eye out for anything out of sorts.

Egan patted Luther's arm and said, "Stay here with me. We need you to keep some distance from the others if the guys shift. They might see you as a threat."

"Okay." Luther leaned against a tree, his attention on us. "I've always wondered what it would be like to watch a shifter change."

"Expect some nudity." Roxy took the bag from Axel and tossed it on the ground. "Their clothes will rip off if they succeed."

"Eh." Luther wrinkled his nose. "Still would be cool. I'll just keep my eyes northbound."

Axel pointed at him. "Good idea."

"Okay, enough kidding around." I enjoyed the friendships we shared, but we had to get these two guys on all fours. They'd come close yesterday, so if I were a betting woman, I'd wager they would get there today. "Get to feeling at one with the earth."

Donovan and Axel closed their eyes. It helped them concentrate, or that was what they thought. As long as it did something, we were good.

I wasn't sure how long we stood there, but suddenly, I heard bones breaking.

Donovan dropped to the ground, and fur sprouted along his arms.

A loud groan left him, and his body contorted. *Holy shit. This hurts.*

I remembered my first shift. It had hurt like a bitch. *The more you shift, the easier it gets. Your body is learning how to do it right now.* I hadn't warned him about the pain in case it scared him from trying to shift. Sometimes, ignorance was bliss.

His shirt ripped off, and his spine molded and transformed as his arms changed to legs.

"He did it," Luther gasped.

Axel followed right behind him, though not quite as far along. His wolf must have been following Donovan's lead. His shift was slower, and by the sounds of it, much more painful.

Their groans turned into cries, which then morphed into howls.

Donovan's pants ripped off, and the last of his bones shifted. A low, threatening growl filled the air, and his eyes locked on Luther.

Shit, maybe we shouldn't have brought him after all.

Before I could react, Donovan ran toward Luther and then lunged aiming for his neck.

CHAPTER NINE

E gan jumped in front of the vampire in the nick of time. He shoved his large hands onto Donovan's shoulders, and the new wolf fell to the ground.

A small whimper left Axel as his body broke the last few bones and completed his transition. I didn't need two unruly wolves running around, unable to control their urges.

Donovan snarled. His animal saw Luther as the ultimate bad guy, probably because a vampire had almost killed them.

Control your wolf. The last thing I wanted to do was use my alpha will on him. He was my equal, but I'd do it if necessary. *Now.*

Fear poured off Donovan and Axel in waves, proving they weren't in their right minds. That was why I'd been afraid of them shifting too soon—they wouldn't be able to control the animal within.

Axel crouched, ready to protect us.

Sadie, you've gotta do something! Roxy yelled through the bond. *They're going to get hurt.*

Or hurt someone, but I somehow kept the words locked in. Roxy wasn't thinking rationally either.

"Donovan. Axel," I said, trying to get their attention on me.

Neither one looked at me. The command had been lacking from my voice.

"You're going to have to do it!" Egan bellowed as the pupils in his golden eyes turned to slits. "Or I'll have to put them down."

Luther scrambled away, making the situation even worse. He was acting like prey and bringing their inner predator closer to the surface.

Donovan stood back on his four legs and watched Luther intently, ready to strike at the first opportunity.

Dammit, they were forcing my hand. I closed my eyes and pulled power from my wolf. I'd never used the alpha will, so I didn't know how to begin. I let my wolf instincts take over. "I said stop it." My voice rang with authority like never before, and the two wolves stopped dead in their tracks. "You will not attack Luther."

Axel whimpered as he tried to disobey me. *Vampire,* he hissed through the pack bond.

Friend, I replied. *They're protecting us. Stop letting your wolf rule you.*

Roxy ran over to stand in front of them, putting herself between Egan and the pack. "They're both our friends. Yes, you need your animal to take over to shift, but not completely. Lock it back down."

Donovan's dark head turned in my direction, and his animal eyes turned a lighter blue as his human side regained control. *Holy shit.* He shook his head hard. *I don't know what happened.*

It's fine. The worse he felt, the harder it would be for

him to trust his wolf in the future. *Your wolf must realize that your human side has slightly more control. That's all.*

But I almost hurt him ... He glanced at Luther.

Next time, he won't be allowed to come. I'd forgotten how volatile the first shift could be. We wouldn't make that mistake again. *Are you okay?*

Yeah. Donovan turned to his friend. *Are you?*

Axel backed away from Egan and Luther. *I was okay after she put the hammer down.*

Donovan lowered his head with shame. *Tell him I'm sorry.*

"Don't try running again," Egan told Luther as he stood with his feet shoulder-width apart, ready for the guys to attack again. "Is everything okay?"

"They're good now," I reassured Egan. If I had to command them again, I wouldn't hesitate. "But you should probably head back to the house." I glanced at the young vampire and lifted a hand toward the wolves. "They need to run around and adapt to their animal forms. I'd hate for something to happen to you."

"No, it's fine." The kid kept his attention on Donovan and Axel. The spicy scent of fear hung in the air. "I'll go back. I only wanted to get out of the house for a little while."

Last night, Katherine had informed us that her brothers weren't strong enough to be around other supernaturals. They didn't like them leaving the house on the off chance they might run into other vampires who might influence them to live like them. She had more control over her humanity and bloodthirst and still almost lost it the night the vampire had nearly drained Donovan and Axel.

"Make sure not to run." Egan puffed his chest bigger. "Their wolves could take over again."

Maybe he was more pufferfish than dragon. At this point, it almost seemed plausible.

"Yeah. Okay." Luther walked off so slowly that a baby could've out crawled him. Poor kid, he might be damaged for life.

"Come on, guys." Roxy waved them after her. "Let me shift, and we'll go for a run."

I wanted to join them, but I wasn't ready yet. Someone needed to stay human with Egan. With the fae and other pack threat so close by, he didn't want us coming out here alone. If we ran into the other pack, I'd need to be able to converse with them. Egan wouldn't know what to say on our behalf.

Are you joining us? Donovan asked with so much hope, but he already knew the answer. We'd talked about it last night.

Nope, but go ahead and have fun. I was excited that they'd gotten this far. Both guys had grown aggravated the past few days when they'd gotten so close to shifting and it hadn't happened. *Bond with your wolf, but make sure he doesn't take too much control.* He needed to be able to shift back to human.

Got it. He walked over and rubbed his body against my legs. *But you know what this means?*

I'll bite. I ran my hand through his soft dark fur, feeling more connected to him than ever.

Exactly. He chuckled, and his tongue rolled out of his mouth. *We're one step closer to biting each other.*

I hadn't meant it like that, but the fact that claiming each other was one of his first thoughts made me fall a little more in love. The past few days had been amazing, and even though we were under threat and facing uncertainty, this was the happiest I'd ever been. It was mainly due to him and the amazing group of people surrounding us.

Roxy ran out from the trees in her wolf form and lowered herself to the ground, playing. She was ready to run and blow off some steam. We'd been cooped up in the house more than normal, trying to keep a low profile.

The three of them took off in a flash, leaving Egan and me behind to scope out the area.

"Let's go outside the vampire's perimeter to ensure they don't come sniffing around." Egan walked toward Titan's pack lands as Roxy and the guys kept to the woods near the house.

A FEW MILES from the pack territory line, Titan's and his wolves' scents hit my nose.

Great, they were already out and about. We'd tried getting an early start to the day so we wouldn't risk running into too many of them.

I patted Egan's arm, but he'd already picked up on them too. He motioned back to the woods, asking if we should retreat.

The strong answer would be no, that we should move forward and face the pack, but I wasn't ready for that. I hadn't sorted out my feelings about my supposed living mother. Maybe Dad had known and that was why he'd treated me the way he had. Maybe it was better to have an adult pretend-daughter than start all over with another female heir.

I nodded, indicating we should leave, but it was too late.

"I was wondering how long it'd take before we ran into each other." Titan stepped from some trees alone.

My wolf nose knew at least ten wolves were hiding behind him. "You've breached your boundary line." Technically, this was still the vampires' side.

"Did you forget that Cassius and I are friendly?" Titan arched an eyebrow as he glanced from me to Egan. "I'm surprised you're with the dragon and not your mate."

"We're friends," Egan responded simply. "Are you too insecure to let your mate hang out with other males?"

It would have been boring without him here with me, that was for sure.

"You better watch it," Titan spoke through clenched teeth. "You may be a dragon, but I am an alpha and should be given some respect."

"Yet, here you are, obviously looking for us." I didn't like it. Now that Winter wasn't here, he'd try to force me to go back with them. *Hey, guys. Where are you?*

We're about two miles from the house, Roxy answered immediately. *Where are y'all? Is it time to shift back?*

No, not yet. I hated to ruin their fun, but they'd be pissed if I didn't alert them to this meeting.

Donovan picked up on my anxiety. *Did you run into that pack?*

Yeah. I refused to lie to him even if I wanted them to continue enjoying themselves. *But I'll let you know if we need backup. As of now, he's just grumbling.*

Nope. Donovan's determination rang clear. *We're on our way.*

There was no point in arguing. They would show up here anyway.

"I wanted a chance to talk to you without Winter around." Titan cracked his knuckles. "You really hurt her by running away without giving her a chance to tell you the whole story."

"So what is this?" Egan gestured behind the alpha. "Are you here to force our hands? If you wanted to talk, it's a little suspect bringing backup."

"Don't worry." Titan lifted his hands in surrender. "They aren't here for that."

"Then why are they?" I wouldn't blindly trust anyone. As soon as we let our guard down, something could happen. "That's some heavy manpower for just talking."

"You never know if something could come off as a threat." The alpha crossed his arms, making it clear that he didn't like being questioned. "Some would say taking precautions is smart."

"As riveting as this conversation is, I'm not interested." He was here to play a dominance game, and my wolf didn't give a shit. Maybe that made me weak, but I didn't care. "If you want something, just say it. Otherwise, we have more important things to do." Like figuring out why the fae had attacked. We still didn't have any leads.

"You're an alpha," Titan said with disgust. "You might want to learn the rules about being one."

"In case you've forgotten, Tyler is my father ..." I stopped myself because, apparently, that could be disputed. "Or, at least, he raised me. If I've learned anything from him, it's how to leverage your own hand and not show your cards. It's about strategy, manipulation, and bullying. If that's what a good alpha stands for, I'm not interested. I'd rather be a weak one."

Titan dropped his arms. "If that doesn't prove you're her daughter, I'm not sure what else would."

"What do you mean?" I wasn't sure if he was complimenting or insulting me. Egan stepped closer to me, ready to come to my defense.

"You're headstrong and determined to lead differently

than the norm." He laughed humorlessly. "Winter's strong like you, but it doesn't matter. I was just hoping you'd talk to her. She's been torn up."

"Oh, well. Her being upset trumps everything." My entire life had been about other people. For just a few days, I'd needed to focus on myself. "It doesn't matter how I'm feeling. For all I know, she's lying."

"You're a wolf." Titan's neck tensed. "You would know if she was lying. Hell, the dragon knows she isn't."

"But the fae ran away awfully fast when you showed up," Egan interjected, proving he had my back. "What if you two are working together?"

"Are you serious?" Titan clenched his hands into fists. "We're the last pack the fae would ever want to work with— if they work with anyone. Do you not realize how elitist that race is?"

"It's not like you'd tell us if you were." Did he think we were stupid? "And why would they be so against working with you as opposed to another pack?" That had been an odd thing to say.

"Maybe if you talked to your mother, you'd under-stand." Titan took a hasty step toward me. "Please, just give her a chance. It would mean the world to her."

Egan moved in front of me, blocking me from Titan's view. "I get you're concerned about your mate, but both parties need to be ready for the discussion. And if Sadie isn't, you need to back the fuck off."

"Look, she's asked us to protect you." Titan pointed at the wolves behind him. "That's why they're here. If she didn't care, why would she have us guarding you?"

"She thinks the fae will return?" Even though I'd phrased it like a question, it wasn't. I agreed. I knew they would be back.

Of course, that was when it would happen.

My head grew dizzy, and I was all too familiar with what it meant. I stumbled, and Egan spun around, catching me before I could hit the ground.

"Sadie?" he asked with concern. "Are they...?"

I shook my head, answering the question he hadn't finished. The last two times I'd felt like this had been around fae, which meant they were near.

A loud howl sounded close by.

Roxy connected with me, her voice almost breaking. *We need your and Egan's help.*

Are they with you? I scanned the area, looking for a threat.

Axel linked with me. *They have Donovan.*

"They're here." I wobbled on my feet, barely able to balance.

"The fae?" Titan asked, but I was already running toward my mate.

CHAPTER TEN

I should've seen it coming. We'd been so focused on Donovan and Axel connecting with their wolves that we'd lost sight of the fae. It wasn't like they wouldn't attack again, but I hadn't been expecting it so soon. We'd been fools.

"You can't run over there with no plan." Titan snatched my arm. "Otherwise, they'll hurt everyone."

He was right, and I hated to admit it. "Fine, but they might take Donovan if we don't get there soon." If I lost him, I wasn't sure who I'd become. He was the only thing grounding me; not even Roxy could do that alone.

"They won't take him." Titan rubbed his hands together. "They plan to use him against you."

Another pained cry echoed from the direction I'd been heading, and my blood ran cold.

There was no way I could stay here. *I'm on my way.* I rushed forward, but Egan stepped in front of me.

We need your help, Axel said, his voice strained. *There are four of them. They have Donovan and trapped Roxy and me in a force field.*

"I'll do a flyover." Egan's wings ripped from his back, tearing yet another shirt off his body. "I'll be right back. Just give me a minute to check for anything that could work to our advantage."

Even though he didn't say it, I could read between the lines. He wanted me to give him that before I did something stupid. "Fine, but hurry. They're in a bad spot," I growled, not completely happy.

"You better be careful," Titan grumbled, unhappy with us not listening to him. "If they see you, they could take you down. The air doesn't give you a huge advantage over them."

"Don't worry." Egan flapped his wings, rising slowly into the sky. "I won't be long." He took off toward the howling.

I respected the dragon, but if he didn't hurry, I wouldn't idly wait for him. Once he got back, we'd be heading toward my pack even if Titan wasn't ready.

Titan said, "More pack members are on the way."

How's everyone holding up? It was a stupid question, but I needed to hear their voices.

We're fine, Donovan assured me. *They aren't hurting us any longer. They're waiting for you, so do not come here.*

Do you really expect me to leave you guys there? The suggestion almost hurt. Did he think that poorly of me?

No, I don't. He sounded less than thrilled. *I just don't want anything to happen to you.*

They'll torture you if I don't come. Either way, they'd make sure I showed. *Egan is scoping out the area while Titan is calling more of his pack.*

Can we trust him? Roxy tried focusing on anything but her fear. *I thought you were afraid he and the fae were working together.*

She was right, but we were screwed either way. *I'm not sure, but we might not have an option.*

I turned my attention back on the alpha. He was pacing in the small area, stealing glances at me every few moments.

He was keeping an eye on me.

If I left preemptively, he might come after me. At least one of us needed to be thinking straight. But the fae wanted me for God knew what reason, and I refused to let my pack suffer because of me.

"Damn, woman," Titan growled and turned his back to me. "She just won't stay back."

I had a feeling I knew who he was talking about: Winter. If he was aggravated with her, his wolf would be more focused on his mate than me. This was my chance.

I quickly and quietly ran deeper into the woods. I felt bad not holding up my end of the bargain with Egan, but he was taking too long.

From several hundred feet away, I heard Titan come back to where I'd been standing.

"You've got to be fucking kidding me," he growled. "Not only is Winter demanding to come, but her daughter runs away at the first opportunity. If I had any doubts they were mother and daughter, they're gone now. Too stubborn for their own good."

Pushing my legs, I hurried faster toward my mate and pack as my heart grew heavy. For Titan to be saying all that under his breath, maybe it wasn't all a lie. I could be dead within minutes and never know the full story about her or me. But I couldn't let my pack get hurt either. That was something I could never survive, so now wasn't the time to focus on the possibility that I might never learn about my true parentage.

The flapping of wings broke through my thoughts as

Egan swooped down in front of me. His face was drawn. "You told me you'd wait for me," he said accusingly.

"I had a chance to sneak away." He knew I didn't trust Titan's pack completely. Winter's story seemed a little convenient. "My pack is getting hurt because of me."

"You're going to get them all killed." Egan placed his hands on my shoulders. "If you care about them, you need to think this through."

"What if Titan—"

"I don't think they're working with the fae." Egan leaned down so we were at eye level. "The fae are a little scrambled and trying to lie low. The wolves can't make a sound anymore. They're forcing them to use the pack bond to communicate with you."

Maybe he was right, but it didn't matter. "We need to get to them."

"We can't do anything just us two." Egan blew out a breath, his usual calm demeanor slipping. "They're too strong. We need all-hands-on-deck."

The pattering of paws pulled my attention from him. Great, Titan and his wolves were on their way. "But—"

"Look, the only chance we have is if they're on our side." Egan lowered his voice before the wolves got into absolute hearing distance. "If we go in now, the five of us won't be able to fend them off."

"Fend them off?" That wasn't far enough. "I wanna kick their asses."

"Down, Cujo," Titan grumbled as he appeared in the clearing. "We've got to see what kind of numbers we're dealing with."

"They said four." I glanced at Egan. "Is that what you saw?"

"No, there are ten of them." Egan frowned. "The other

six are hiding in the woods to throw us off. There could be more than that, though."

"Did they not see you flying by?" They were likely aware that we knew their numbers. "Aren't they in tune and all that?"

"I kept low and a good distance away." Egan stared the alpha down. "They had no clue. I'm sure of it."

"Now listen here, we're doing things my—" Titan started, but Winter stepped into view, her long hair in a ponytail and her face set with determination.

"He's a dragon." Winter tensed when she stopped beside me. "If he says he wasn't detected, he wasn't."

"I told you to stay back at the house." Titan didn't bother to pretend to be angry. "Why are you here?"

"To get Sadie." She took my arm and tugged me toward their pack. "She needs to be with me."

"Oh, hell no." That wasn't happening. "I'm part of this. My pack and mate have been captured. I'm not running to safety while their lives are on the line."

"They took them to get to you." Winter exhaled in frustration. "That's why you shouldn't be there."

"There's no way I'm leaving them." I yanked my arm from her grasp and took off running toward the fae. The longer I stayed away, the more at risk my pack was.

"Now you know how it feels," Titan whispered behind me.

The group ran behind me, keeping pace. From what I could tell, there were thirty wolves from Titan's pack, excluding him and Winter. I could only hope that was enough to fight off all of the fae.

Sadie, they know you're close. Donovan's voice shook with concern. *Be careful.*

Are you three still okay? I needed to make sure they weren't injured.

Yeah, they haven't done anything to us yet, Roxy reassured even though it fell flat. *They're being oddly patient.*

I was sure they were. I didn't want to risk speaking out loud now that we were so close. The fae's floral scent hit my nose in waves. I slowed to a walk as I passed through the last line of small trees that hid me.

"There she is." An elegant voice said with a hint of an accent. It wasn't quite British but similar. "Our guest of honor has arrived."

My eyes focused first on Donovan. He was still in wolf form and standing next to a man close to my height.

The fae's long green hair floated in the breeze. His skin had a yellow hue similar to the yellow-haired fae beside him, the same fae who had attacked us. Roxy and Axel sat on his other side.

They were also in wolf form. It took me a second to notice the semi-glowing, transparent cage wrapped around them. The power radiating off it hit me in my core.

"What do you want?" Obviously, they were after something.

"To know what you are." The green-haired one stepped closer to Donovan and squatted next to him. "We tried talking to you last time and didn't have much luck, so we thought this strategy might work better." He snaked his fingers into Donovan's fur.

"You attacked us. That was a strange way to start a conversation."

"We need you to come with us," the yellow-haired one interjected like he was afraid he'd be ignored. "As soon as you do, we'll let your *pack* go." He said the word like it disgusted him.

"There's no chance in hell that's happening." Winter stepped beside me and stared down the fae. "Why don't you let the wolves go and be on your merry way?"

"Now, that isn't a possibility." The green-haired one arched an eyebrow. "I'd reconsider starting something you can't handle."

"We're good." Egan appeared on my other side. "Let them go or there will be consequences." He breathed raggedly, ready to fight.

"They can't say we didn't warn them." The green-haired one lifted a hand, and a spark of light sped across the clearing toward us.

I dropped to the ground, narrowly avoiding the light. Something huge hit the ground behind me.

Four wolves lunged forward and attacked the green-haired fae, causing him to drop his focus from me.

My eyes went to where the light had hit right behind me, and I found a tree sliced right down the center. The top half had fallen over.

They hadn't started the fight half-heartedly. They had struck to kill.

More fae ran from the woods as Egan had warned us. There were ten to our thirty-seven, but unfortunately, it seemed like an uneven battle since the fae were naturally more powerful than wolves when they initially arrived on Earth.

Titan's pack charged at the fae, leaving my pack wide open.

The fae weren't trying to harm the wolves like they had tried to harm me, which I found so odd. I would talk to Winter about this when it was over. It was time I put my stubbornness aside.

I raced toward Donovan, and Egan followed my lead,

heading to Axel and Roxy. I wasn't sure what the hell to do, but there had to be a way to get them out.

Sadie, I don't know how to get out of here. Donovan stood on all fours but hit his head on the ceiling. *I have no clue how they're keeping me in.*

It had something to do with nature or energy. *Does it hurt when you touch it?*

No. He shook his wolf head. *But I can't tell what it is.*

I touched it, and the magic vibrated deep inside me. What strange magic was this? How did it almost feel like part of me?

Are you okay? Donovan's voice pulled me from my daze.

Yeah. I closed my eyes, letting whatever was inside me take over. That had to be the key, right? *Give me a second.* Something churned inside me, and static electricity overtook me once more. It funneled into my hand and zapped from my fingers.

The resistance vanished. *Try it now.*

Donovan jumped to his feet and shook his entire body. *It worked. What the hell?*

A fae gestured toward me. "Look at what she did."

"How the...?" The green fae frowned and pushed two wolves off him and into a large tree. "You're—" Before he could finish that comment, Winter charged him, growing her claws, and sank them into his arm.

"Agh!" the green fae yelled and grabbed Winter around the neck.

Titan was there in a flash. "No, you don't." He punched the fae hard in the face, and light pink blood poured out of his nose.

"There are too many of them," a fae near Egan said. "And it smells like vamps."

"Dammit." The green fae stumbled back and pinched his nose. "They're going to outnumber us again."

"We'd better go." The yellow-haired one vanished from sight.

"We won't make the same mistake twice," the green-haired one snarled and stared at me with hatred before turning to Titan. "You'd better get your affairs in order because, next time, this will end at any cost."

And just like that, all of the fae were gone.

I fell down and wrapped my arms around Donovan. He licked my face, and I smiled.

Thank God you're safe. I buried my face in his neck, breathing in his musky, rainy scent. I hated that I'd gotten him all wrapped up in this. *I love you so much.*

I love you too, he almost purred.

"Are you okay?" Winter squatted next to me. "Did you get hurt?"

"No, I'm fine." I took a deep breath, realizing I'd been so stupid. By not facing the truth, I'd potentially put us in more danger. "But I think it's time to be honest and answer some questions, even the ones you won't like."

CHAPTER ELEVEN

Something unreadable passed through Winter's eyes. "Okay." Her voice lacked the thrill from before.

She knew I would ask things she didn't want to answer. Maybe she'd been foolish to think she'd only have to tell me the parts she wanted me to know, but that wouldn't cut it.

People became uncomfortable when someone wanted to learn both sides of the story, but that was the only way to really learn the truth. Because the truth usually was somewhere between the two tales. Not just one person's version but everyone's. The truth seldom painted anyone in the best light when looked at from all sides. No decision or action was ever perfect, and we all had our own hidden agendas. Hell, a person could even paint Roxy and me as villains for forcing a life upon Donovan and Axel that they hadn't accepted or asked for. We'd saved them, sure, but we'd also done it because we didn't want to live without them.

Are you sure now is the time for this conversation? Donovan asked as I focused on Egan and the rest of my pack.

We have to know what we're up against. If facing the

truth could put us on even ground with the fae and Tyler, then it was worth hearing. *Otherwise, someone will get hurt or worse.*

Some help would be appreciated here, Roxy whined and pawed at the ground. *Dragon boy can't get us out. Isn't he originally from the fae world?*

I walked past Winter and headed straight to them. *Hey, he's trying, so don't give him hell.*

Egan's hands shook as he clutched the bars of the force field, veins bulging in his arms. He groaned, and his face turned red from the strain. It looked like he was trying to force out a poop. After a second, he blew out a breath. He looked so defeated. "I can't get them out. Can you?"

"I'm hoping so." I prayed whatever was inside me would reveal itself again. "Let me try." I touched the barrier with both hands and closed my eyes. I wasn't sure how I'd managed it before, but nothing stirred inside me. "Dammit."

Cassius and the rest of the nest raced into the clearing, ready to attack. Dawn was on one side of him and Lillith on the other. Katherine stood beside Lillith with her parents and brothers right behind. Cassius, Paul, and Athan held guns while Luther held a bow and arrow. The women had knives, prepared for an attack.

When the elder vampire saw we weren't fighting, his body relaxed marginally. "It appears the fae have already left. Is everyone all right?"

"Yeah, they left moments ago. Thanks for coming so quickly," Titan grumbled behind me. "None of us sustained any serious injuries, but we need to free those two."

Titan must have had someone from his pack go get the vampires. My attention turned back to my pack members I was struggling to free.

Can I help? Donovan leaned against my leg, comforting me.

No, but I don't know how the hell I got you out. I needed a repeat performance, pronto. *It just happened, and I can't recreate it.*

"They look fine." Lillith walked over and reached for them, but her hand landed on the force field. "What the...? Is that a barrier?" She pushed her hand against it, but it didn't budge. "That's weird. I can't feel anything, but something is holding me back, and it's invisible."

"Has anyone had luck with something like this before?" Katherine stood beside Lillith and squinted at the force-field. "I don't see a damn thing."

"It's some sort of transparent cage the fae have wrapped around them." I didn't know how else to describe it.

"Sadie got Donovan out, but she's struggling now." Egan rubbed his chin. "Maybe it's because the fae aren't threatening you anymore. Maybe you need something like an inciting event."

"Maybe." Did I work better under pressure? Or was the magic inside me activated under high stress?

"Try to push deeper." Winter stepped behind me and placed a hand on my shoulder. "It's in your blood."

"What do you mean?" The answer was clear, but I was too scared to consider it. It'd been nagging me for days, but I'd kept pushing away the possibility. However, today was a new day, and I was done running.

"I tried to tell you the other day," Winter said as she pulled my shoulder, causing me to turn to face her. "Tyler isn't your father."

"Can you stop?" Lillith pointed at Roxy and Axel. "We need to get them out of here, not have family story time. The fae could come back to finish the job."

She was right, but I had nothing to work with.

"It's relevant at the moment." Winter met my gaze. "She's the only one who can get them out of there." She paused and stared at the ground like she was searching for the strength within. When she finally looked at me again, I knew her next words would change my future forever. I wouldn't be denying it any longer. "Your father was fae."

Maybe that should have shocked me, wrecked me even, but it didn't. I'd already known this deep inside me, and the words resonated in a way that both made sense but also made things more confusing.

That was why I'd felt a connection with the fae in the bathroom back at Kortright. Why I had rose-gold hair, which was never seen before in the shifter community. Why I could feel the fae when they transported here and whatever magic churned inside me.

The surge of emotions overwhelmed me. I didn't understand the thoughts and feelings.

Cassius sounded shocked as he said, "You've got to be joking. That's impossible."

"Unfortunately, she's not." Titan seemed even less thrilled. "This is one reason we're hiding here."

Their reactions mixed with my already raging feelings and pushed me closer to the edge. The magic rumbled, the static electricity taking hold again. The magic was tied to my emotions, which was extremely problematic and volatile. That was exactly what Roxy and I had been training the boys out of with their wolves.

I needed whatever charged it. I closed my eyes and focused on the barrier in front of me.

"Sadie ..." Egan started, but I held a hand up before latching onto the barrier.

I needed to use the energy productively while I had it.

Electricity thrummed throughout me. It was so damn intense I'd bet my hair stood on end. That was how raw it made me feel. I tapped into the magic, and fortunately, it worked like it had with Donovan.

The magic pushed through my body toward my hands and poured into the barrier. The force shocked me, but whatever held them evaporated. "There." I dropped my hands to my sides and ignored the power still pulsing inside me. I had nowhere to direct it other than inward. I refused to risk hurting anyone here.

Roxy stood on all fours while Axel stretched out.

Dude, being squashed sucks. Axel whimpered. *I can't imagine living in a cage.*

I can agree with that. Donovan's guilt flowed through the bond. *I feel bad for all those pets we had growing up.*

Don't, Axel said, attempting to comfort him. *They were our foster parents' pets, not ours.*

"You ready to come back with us?" Winter glanced from my pack back to me. "Since you want to talk and all?"

There was no way in hell I was going back to Titan's pack and potentially getting stuck there. "How about you come back to Cassius's?" I had a feeling Titan wouldn't let her come alone.

Winter nibbled on her lip. "Don't we want some privacy?"

"Uh ..." Titan tensed. "I'm coming along."

"Donovan needs to change, and I'm sure Egan could keep Titan busy with research or something." I wanted to be on familiar grounds, but I hated to take advantage of the vampires' hospitality by inviting people over. "It is a huge-ass house."

"Sure, you can use the library," Lillith jumped in,

having my back. "Tons of old books, and it's even soundproof."

Ew ... Roxy linked with me. *Does Cassius have a librarian fetish?*

A smile spread across my face, and I couldn't hold back my snort. *I'm sure you're the only one who had that thought.*

Although ... Axel interjected. *That does sound interesting. Maybe—*

No. Donovan grimaced, even in wolf form. *Stop. We don't want to hear it.*

I agreed and pushed the inappropriate conversation out of my mind. I turned my attention to Cassius and Dawn. "If that's okay with you." They'd done so much that I needed to at least get their blessing first.

"It's your home too." Dawn smiled comfortingly. "Of course, you can use the library."

"Okay, then." Winter shrugged, giving in. "That's fine. Let's go."

Titan scowled, clearly not happy. "But if there's one disrespectful thing said ..."

I understood his concern. He already thought I'd been unnecessarily cruel to Winter. "Then you'd be more than welcome to leave." I wouldn't let him bully or force me into behaving differently, even if his intent was to protect his mate. "Unlike us heading to your pack, we won't force you to stay against your will."

Titan's nostrils flared as his face turned pink. "Now listen here—"

"Stop it." Winter placed a hand on his shoulder. "If that's where she wants to have the conversation, that's where we'll go. Besides, you and Cassius have worked together for years. You know we can trust him."

"He's not the problem." Titan's eyes shot daggers at me.

"I'm more worried about the girl who has influence over you."

"That girl is my daughter." Winter pointed her finger in Titan's face. "And if she wants to talk to me, I will listen. If you're going to cause a problem, I can come back home when we're done and I'm ready."

The alpha's shoulders hunched, and he sighed. "Fine, but I will force you to leave if it goes south." He touched her arm, but his eyes remained sincere. "Even if I must use the alpha will."

He didn't trust me. Well, the feeling was mutual. At least, we had something in common. "Let's go. No reason to stay out here like targets."

"I'll catch up." Titan gestured to his pack. "Let me handle a few things." He turned and headed over to his wolves.

I'll head back and change. Donovan trotted off but slowed. *I want to be ready in case you need me when the conversation goes down.*

I somehow fell more in love with him since he wasn't forcing his presence on the conversation. *Please stay close. I don't want you getting attacked without backup again.*

He paused and waited for me to catch up to him. Soon, the nest, my pack, Egan, and Winter all headed back toward the mansion.

The entire walk back happened in complete silence. Every single one of us was on edge, afraid that the fae might pop up again. Luckily, during the trek back, nothing out of the ordinary happened. We'd grabbed the bag of clothing on the way back, and as soon as we made it to the back porch, I handed it to Lillith to take up to our rooms. Donovan, Roxy, and Axel ran inside behind her, ready to get changed.

"Let's go put up our supplies," Cassius said as he lifted his guns.

The rest followed after him, leaving me, Winter, and Egan on the back porch, waiting for Titan.

"Thank you for helping us today." Egan gave her a small smile. He stepped toward the door before stopping again. He cracked his knuckles and caught my eye, asking me an unspoken question. He wasn't sure whether he should leave me alone with her or not.

I nodded, telling him it was okay.

"You're welcome." Winter smiled sadly. "A friend of Sadie's is a friend of mine."

Titan appeared from the tree line with a large frown on his face. He joined us on the back porch and looked at his mate. "Maybe I should stay out here with you."

"No, go on to the library." Winter straightened her shoulders, leaving no room for argument. "I'll let you know if I need you."

Egan opened the back door into the kitchen. "Cassius and Dawn have been combing through the library for a way to defeat the fae and found a few books they want to go over with us. It's like the answer is in code."

"You know those fae are tricky sons of bitches." Titan stepped into the house and shut the door, leaving me and Winter alone.

We stared toward the woods, not knowing how to begin. If she was my mother, wouldn't this be natural?

She inhaled sharply. "First off, I just want to say it means the world to me to find out—"

"Just stop." I didn't want to hear how she was happy or how she hoped we could make up for lost time. I wasn't interested in any of that. "I want to know who my father is.

Does he know about me?" He was probably another dead-beat dad who didn't want to protect his daughter.

"No, he didn't know about you." Winter's voice soft-ened with regret.

"Didn't?" That sounded so final. "Is he dead?" That would be my luck.

"Yes, he is."

Winter reached out to touch me, but I stepped back and countered the movement, letting her hand fall. I wasn't trying to be a heartless bitch, but I had my own emotions to deal with. "He never knew about me? You left and didn't tell him?"

"No, no." Winter lifted a hand. "Just give me a second to explain."

I nodded and didn't say anything else, hoping to encourage her to continue.

"I grew up in Tyler's pack." She paused and huffed. "Well, his father's pack at the time. I was one of the strongest females they'd ever had, which made Tyler want me. Obviously, the two of us together would make an even stronger heir."

"Okay."

"You see, they didn't give me an option." She stepped back and leaned against the brick wall. "I was informed at fourteen that I'd been promised. Even if I found my fated mate, it wouldn't matter. I was to sacrifice everything for my pack."

"Even a fated mate?" Fated mates trumped everything, but I could see Tyler thinking he was above that.

"Yes, and I had to agree." Mom shivered. "They threat-ened my parents."

I bet they had. What Tyler wanted, Tyler got. He didn't

care who he had to screw over. "How did the fae get involved?"

"I told them I had to go off to college." Winter ran a hand through her hair and sighed. "That was my condition if I had to give up a fated mate. They agreed. It was a local community college, but a fae also attended there. We had some classes together and started dating."

"Even though you were promised?" That had obviously been a terrible idea. "And I thought fae were forbidden to date outside their race."

"We'd never been attracted to someone before, and we were each promised to someone we didn't want." Mom placed a hand on her chest at the memory. "It was only meant to be a friendship, and it turned into so much more."

"And I'm assuming Dad found out?" I grimaced at calling him *dad*. It felt wrong to call Tyler that when we were talking about my actual father.

"Tyler did." She nodded, ignoring my mistake. "It was right after Rook and I had sex. He found us at Rook's temporary apartment."

Gross. I got that sex had been required to make me, but I still didn't want to visualize that with her.

"He brought a special knife and five other pack members." Winter sniffled as she stared off, lost in memories. "They burst through the doors. Luckily, we were in the kitchen, getting something to eat. Tyler grabbed me and put a knife to my throat. He made Rook stand down to save me. Then a pack member took the knife and stabbed Rook in the heart. He died right in front of me."

I couldn't even fathom someone killing another person like that. It seemed so cold. Rook hadn't deserved that. Out of everyone, he'd been the most innocent, but it proved that Dad had been a narcissistic asshole even back then. "What happened after that?" I needed to hear it even if I knew how the rest happened.

"Tyler forced me back to the pack." Winter wrapped her arms around herself. "He threatened my family, so we consummated the promise that night, and a few weeks later, I found out I was pregnant with you."

And here was the question I really wanted to know the answer to. "Does he know?"

"No, Tyler thinks you're his." Winter met my eyes once more. "The alternative never crossed his mind even with your rose-gold hair. He would've thrown it in my face otherwise. And had he figured it out, you wouldn't be standing here. He wouldn't have allowed you to live."

I'd hoped for that answer, but it left me cold. There was still one thing I really needed to know, and I hoped she'd answer me the way I needed her to.

CHAPTER TWELVE

I turned to face Winter, wanting to see her reaction. "How could you leave without confirming I was really dead?" The whole believing the maid that I was dead was a little too far-fetched.

She pursed her lips and fidgeted. "You have to understand." She pushed off the wall and stepped closer to me. "I was young."

"That excuse doesn't work." Blaming youth was a cop-out. Maybe she hadn't made the best decisions, but she would have to face the consequences with me. "I want to know why."

"Okay." She nodded. "I was eighteen ..."

"Again, that excuse won't work with me." Maybe I was being rude, but I didn't give a flying fuck. Her age was irrel-evant. I deserved to know the whole truth and not the story she told herself to sleep better at night. "I need the facts outside of your age. I realize how young you were. No reminder needed."

"Fine." She huffed and met my gaze. "Then, let me explain how I was forced into a relationship with a man I hated and who killed my first love right in front of me. We were supposed to be mated weeks after Rook had died, but when he found out I was pregnant, I got him to put it off. I pretended to have severe morning sickness."

Great, so she had used me to her advantage even before I was born. "And he couldn't tell you weren't sick?" There was a foulness to the air when someone was actually ill. It was something a wolf could call bullshit on.

"I was sick, so it wasn't a lie, but it wasn't because of you." She shivered. "It was guilt, and I was mourning Rook, but if Tyler had known it was related to that, the mating ceremony wouldn't have been postponed."

"You were safe while pregnant with me." It made sense, kind of. "That doesn't seem like something Dad would do, though. He's not known for his caring spirit."

"I told him I might get nauseous and puke during the ceremony." Winter snorted, the corners of her mouth tilting upward. "You know the type of people who would have shown up at that ceremony."

"The top elites of the supernatural races." He'd want to gloat that he was mating a strong female wolf he could control. It would have strengthened his family's status. "So, puking would be frowned upon."

"Exactly." She rubbed her belly as if she were living in the past. "It was pushed to two weeks after your due date."

"Not right after?" I figured he'd be gunning for it as soon as I'd popped out.

"I had to have time to slim back down to my pre-pregnancy form," she said bitterly. "He couldn't have a cow in a wedding dress."

"That sounds like a direct quote." Dad had a way with words.

"Oh, it is." She dropped her hands to her sides and

faced me again. "But there was more anxiety than from those reasons. You see, I felt something strange while pregnant with you."

"Strange?" I hadn't heard pregnancy called that before, but I guessed it worked. "Like with a small person inside you?"

"No, like I felt connected with nature." She walked onto the grass and began to pace. "It was something I'd never experienced before, and that's when fear overtook me."

"You had an inkling that Rook was my real dad." That had to be it. From what I understood, fae were part of nature, and shifters lived in it. "Is that when you knew?"

"No, not at first." She turned her back to me. "I thought maybe it was the fae coming to kill me. Rook and I having sex was frowned upon, and I figured his fiancée might want to settle the price of his life."

Ew ... she was talking about sex again. Even if we didn't have the normal mother-daughter bond, there were still some things I didn't want to hear. However, there were more important things to focus on.

"Are the fae that vindictive?" Being part fae, I hoped to connect with that side someday if they didn't kill me first.

"Oh, sweetheart," she said. "They are. You need to wrap your head around that. They care about their race and their kind only. Rook always complained about it. He thought it was an outdated notion."

"That's lovely." I'd never get to know that part of myself truly, only what I could figure out on my own. At least, I had Egan, who could provide some guidance. "But I'm part fae." I was part of their race.

Winter frowned. "But not full-blooded. It doesn't count to them. I'm sorry."

"Of course it doesn't." Why would this race be any different from Dad's family? "Please, go on."

"After several weeks, when the fae never revealed themselves, I knew. The magic had to be coming from inside me ... from you. You weren't Tyler's." She chuckled without humor. "Which was a blessing."

"You weren't scared he might figure it out?" Her logic wasn't the most sound. "That my life could be on the line?" If that'd been me, I'd have done anything to protect my daughter. What was wrong with people?

"Oh, I was, and it made me sicker. That's one reason why you came early." She picked at her nail, avoiding my gaze. "The night I went into labor with you, I knew my time was truly ticking down. For some reason, your birth made it even more real."

And here I'd thought having a baby was a time for celebration. "I'm sorry I was such an inconvenience to you." Sarcasm and disgust laced my words. There wasn't a way to hide how much that hurt.

"That's not what I meant." She pinched the bridge of her nose. "I was thrilled to have you. You weren't the problem."

I didn't bother to respond. If she wanted me to comfort her, it wouldn't happen. I was the one who'd been left behind and raised by a tyrant.

"You're asking for the truth, and I'm giving it to you." She scowled. "Do you want me to continue?"

She had me there. "Please, continue." I almost winced, not sure if I meant it, but the blinders had to come off.

"The jackass demanded to be in the delivery room." She stood in front of me, rocking on her feet. "I wanted to see you first. I prayed I was paranoid and that you were, in fact, not fae. If you were, I wasn't sure how the hell I could protect you."

"How was him not being in the room going to protect me better?" That didn't make any sense. "I'm not following."

"I was scared. You—" She cut off mid-word. "I mean ... I wasn't thinking with a clear mind. I wanted to have a few minutes to come up with a plan."

"But that didn't happen."

"No, he refused." She stilled. "When you were delivered, my heart stopped when I saw your light pink hair."

"I'm not sure how he didn't suspect I wasn't his." Maybe I was missing a huge piece of information. Tyler wasn't stupid.

"Roxy was born a few weeks before you with that vibrant red hair." Winter glanced over her shoulder at the house. "It caused a slight commotion in the pack, seeing as red is very rare among our kind. That's when it came to light that a witch might have cursed our pack."

"What?" I'd never heard that before. "A witch cursed us? That doesn't seem likely." People seldom rose up against Dad.

"It was when Tyler was taking over the supernatural scene and angering some people. A brave witch decided to make our pack look weak by creating what some might consider deformities. She didn't do anything physical because she didn't want to hurt the sweet, innocent children. It was only meant to make Tyler and the pack look undesirable."

"Is that why Roxy got treated so poorly?" Could my best friend be stronger than what we'd perceived? "But how did I come out unscathed? Shouldn't I have been viewed the same way?"

"It was a blessing that Tyler assumed the witch had done that to you." She winced. "Well, maybe not a blessing, but when he saw you, he came unglued."

I bet he did. He despised losing control. "But the witch would have already been dealt with after what she did to Roxy."

"Not exactly," Winter said with disgust. "They locked the witch in a cell and tried to find out who helped her. She insisted she'd worked alone, but they didn't believe her. When Tyler saw you ..."

"He killed her, didn't he?" It would have infuriated him that someone had made him look stupid or unfit to lead. "Are you sure my pink hair isn't from her?" Maybe this was all a big misunderstanding and I wasn't fae after all. I wasn't sure if I was hoping that was the case or not.

"Honey, you took down that fae barrier." Winter lifted an eyebrow. "And from what Cassius told Titan, you've teleported and stuff. You're fae."

"But ...did you have doubts?" Maybe that was why she hadn't thought twice about leaving me.

"No. Your pink hair is the exact same as Rook's mother." She smiled tenderly. "He showed me a picture once when he was homesick, and your hair and angular face match her dead on."

Hearing that made the truth about Rook more real. Not only did I have a dad I'd never get to meet, but I had grandparents and family who might have liked to know me. Even that right had been stripped away. "Does she know about me?" My voice sounded small, which pissed me off.

"I'm sorry, but no." Winter touched my shoulder. "Your father died before he knew about you, and it's not like I can get in touch with the fae."

"What about your parents?" Could I at least have one

set of grandparents who might want to know me? Dad—I meant Tyler. Damn, it felt strange calling him by his real name, but it also felt weird continuing to call him Dad. Tyler's parents had died shortly after my birth, and he'd taken over the pack. The rumor was Tyler had killed them, but no one was brave enough to accuse him.

"I told my parents my plan to run away. They were ready." Winter inched a little closer. "They're part of Titan's pack now and live with the others. That's another reason I've been trying to bring you there. They're dying to meet you."

Hope and fear ran rampant inside me. That was just another thing to consider while I sorted through how the hell I felt about everything. I'd definitely need to process that piece later.

We were digressing. I needed to hear the rest of the story. "Okay, so he thinks I have pink hair because of a witch's curse. Why didn't the pack treat me like Roxy?"

"After Tyler killed the witch, he cleaned himself up and called all the supernatural leaders on Earth to inform them that his child had been born and she held the sign that he was one of the strongest supernaturals in the world. He said he'd dreamed that he'd have a pink-haired daughter and she would bear the strongest wolf shifter in the world."

"He believes that?" You'd have thought he'd have been a little nicer to me if he thought that.

"God, no." Winter shook her head. "But he had to put your uniqueness in a good light. No one dared to challenge him. Everyone knew what happened when you went up against his family. So they accepted it, and you were treated like a normal wolf shifter."

"If by normal you mean insulted and put down at every opportunity he had, then sure." He'd treated me so poorly my entire life, and I'd allowed it. At least the cycle was finally ending even if I had to forfeit my life.

"I'm sorry. I had no clue." She exhaled. "It was a few nights before the mating ceremony, and I knew I had to get out of there. He'd kept my room heavily guarded, but he was going out of town and pulled a few men off my room. I knew it was my one and only chance to escape."

I couldn't fault her for that. I'd never want to mate with someone like Tyler. Once you sealed the bond, it was done. Even if you found your fated mate only death could sever it. That was why shifters had to be sure they were okay with mating before committing to each other.

"I waited until he'd left the premises." Her eyes filled with pain. "It took longer than normal, which should've been my first clue."

"You already told me this part." I didn't need to hear it again. "You ran into the maid, and she told you I'd died and Tyler had taken off with me. But why didn't you check before you left? That's what I want to know." I tried to hide the pain from my voice, but it leaked through.

"Because I thought he'd figured out you weren't his and that he'd kill me." She cast her eyes to the ground, looking ashamed. "My survival instincts kicked in, and I ran. When I saw you a week ago, I knew I'd made the biggest mistake of my life."

"At least, you're honest." She'd assumed I'd died so she could move on and live. It wasn't a pretty truth, but it was true. There wasn't the smell of a lie, and her pain seemed genuine. Somehow, that made it worse.

"Does that mean we can build a relationship?" she asked with so much damn hope.

"I'm not sure what you mean." If she was expecting us to hold hands and skip in the sunshine, that was a hard no.

"But I'm open to working together to protect your pack, my pack, and my friends." I hadn't wanted to collaborate with them before. I wasn't thrilled about it now, but surviving was a big deal.

"We can get to know each other, right?"

"I'm not ready for that." I hated this whole situation, and everything I came into contact with turned out messy. What had I ever done to make fate hate me so?

Donovan linked with me, feeling the turmoil through our bond. *Are you okay?*

Define okay?

"I get that it will take time ..." she pushed.

I need you. I got that she wanted to find redemption, forgiveness, or, hell, maybe even peace, but I wasn't in the right place for that.

I'm on my way.

"Look, we had the talk you wanted." I waved my hand between us. "And our packs need to work together, but that's all I can commit to." I was barely holding it together. My biological father was dead. His side of the family knew nothing about me—but even if they did, they'd want me dead—my mother had abandoned me, and Tyler had treated me worse than scum.

"No, I get that, but I was hoping—"

The back door opened, cutting her off, and I almost cried when Donovan stepped outside. His blue eyes darkened with concern, and his dark hair was messy. His presence already provided some comfort.

Winter glared, unhappy with the interruption.

Unfazed, he walked over to me and wrapped an arm around my waist. "How's everyone doing out here?"

"We are in the middle of a conversation."

"Actually, we are done." I met her gaze directly. I'd dealt

with as much as I was willing to and needed time to figure out my feelings. "But thank you for your honesty."

She pouted. "But Titan isn't out here."

"I'm sure you can find him in the library." Donovan stood strong beside me. "They probably need extra help. I'm thinking after what Sadie went through, a nap would do her good."

In our brief time together, he already knew how I worked. "I am exhausted." Really, I wanted to be alone and not be afraid to fall apart.

He opened the door. "There's no time like the present."

I entered the kitchen, and Winter followed behind.

"Hey." Katherine pulled out a bag of blood from the refrigerator. "Titan asked me to come get you and take you to the library."

"Well, here she is." The sooner I got some distance, the better. My emotions were all over the place.

"Well, alrighty then." Katherine smiled.

"Okay, I'll see you later." I glanced at Winter and then exited the kitchen, heading to the stairs.

As I passed by the den, Roxy jumped up from the couch where she'd been sitting next to Axel. Her eyes landed on me, and she said over her shoulder to Axel, "I'm going upstairs for a minute."

"Do I need to go with you?" Axel asked as he followed her gaze.

"Nope, we're good." She headed over to me and waved Axel off. "Just kick Luther's ass in the game."

She didn't say anything as the three of us headed upstairs and into Donovan's and my bedroom. When the door shut behind me, my shoulders sagged as I gave in to my emotions.

"Hey, are you okay?" Roxy pulled me into a hug. "That had to be a hard conversation."

"I'll be all right." I returned her embrace and pulled back, taking Donovan's hand. The way they supported me meant the world to me. "Especially with the two of you by my side."

"You know I'll always have your back." Her hazel eyes turned a deep brown. "No matter what, you'll always be my girl."

"I know." She had been the one constant. She'd had my back when no one else had. "And I love you."

"I love you too."

"What the hell, man!" Axel yelled from downstairs. "You're cheating."

"It's not cheating when someone is better than you," the normally quiet vampire shot back.

"Okay, I better get back down there." She rolled her eyes. "Boys and their games." She pointed at Donovan. "Am I good leaving my girl in your care?"

"I'll always take care of her," Donovan promised in a low, raspy voice that warmed my body.

"Good." She gave me another quick hug and walked out the door, shutting it behind her.

"Come here." Donovan climbed into bed and opened his arms wide.

I happily obliged and nestled my head into his chest, listening to his heartbeat. I closed my eyes, trying to melt into his embrace and find comfort in his arms, but something nagged at my brain that I couldn't ignore.

CHAPTER THIRTEEN

"**D**o you think I'm being too hard on her?" I wasn't willing to open up to Winter yet, but I needed to know if I was acting like a completely unjustified ass.

"Who?" Donovan's fingertips brushed my arm as he chuckled. "Winter?"

I smacked him on the arm gently. "Yes. Who else would I be talking about?"

"In all fairness, you're super hard on yourself." Donovan pulled me closer to him. "But to answer your question, no, you aren't being too hard on her."

"Then, why do I feel like I am?" I'd always wanted to know my mother. I'd dreamed of her so many times growing up. I'd imagined her coming to me and taking me away from Tyler. Wasn't that what mothers were supposed to do? Protect their children at all costs? She hadn't done any of that for me.

"Because you grew up thinking she was dead." He kissed my forehead. "And then you found out what happened, which was almost worse. She was alive and left you behind even if it was unintentional."

When he put it like that, my anger, my hesitancy, and even my longing made more sense. However, the first two feelings were the strongest, which made me even angrier for wanting to know her more. Blood didn't create a family. I had to remind myself of that.

"What do I do?" I didn't know how to move forward. How did you overcome something like that? Inside, my feelings lay shattered.

"You discover yourself first."

It sounded so simple. And the truth behind it rocked me to my core.

I didn't know who I was.

My entire life, Tyler had dictated so much. Hell, at times, I'd felt like I wasn't allowed to breathe without permission. Then, Brock had jumped at the opportunity to attend Kortright University with me, and he was just as bad as Tyler. Brock had smothered me and tried to control me, despite being from a different pack. "How do I do that?"

"You take things day by day." He intertwined our fingers. "You don't have to figure everything out today."

"I just don't want to live with a lifetime of guilt if something bad happens." I moved back to look him in the eyes. "Not only to my mom but to you too." The whole day was catching up to me in a flash. "You got captured because of me."

"But I didn't get hurt," he reassured me.

"No, but you could've." Everyone I was close to seemed to have a target on their backs. Roxy had taken on more hostility and pettiness from Tyler than she would've if we hadn't been friends, and a vampire had targeted Donovan. Was I cursed? "Those fae used each one of you to get to me. They separated you. They have to know you're my mate."

"It doesn't matter." Emotion laced each word. "There is

nowhere else I want to be than here with you. I'm okay with the risks."

"I'm not sure I am." The thought of him dying hurt so much. That was why I'd bitten him in the first place. "You deserve to be happy—"

He kissed me, cutting off my words. *I'm the happiest I've ever been. There's no getting rid of me.*

It's not that I want to get rid of you. I should have pulled back. He was trying to distract me, but the distraction was too enticing. *I just want to protect you. What was the point of changing you if you're going to wind up hurt anyway?*

Sadie, he warned and ended our kiss. "I get that I was an ass after you changed me, but I felt so different and strange. I didn't have control over my emotions."

"I'm not trying to make you feel bad." This conversation was heading in a different direction than I'd intended. "I get that."

"Let me finish," he growled. "Can you do that for me?"

I wanted to say "bite me," but he had a right to say what he wanted. "Fine. But I can't promise I won't interrupt."

"Clearly." He rolled his eyes. "Should I get a muzzle?"

"Not funny." I tried to stop the smile from peeking through, but I must have failed because he smirked with pride.

"But seriously." His mouth straightened, and his face filled with adoration. "I'm so damn glad you changed me. What we have is stronger because of it, and I've never been this happy."

"Even with all the death threats?" I challenged. Normally, that would have been a deal-breaker.

"Yes." Donovan tangled his fingers in my hair. "For the first time, I feel like I belong. Before, I always felt strange in my skin."

"It was probably your wolf." That was one reason supernaturals tended to date within their own race. It wasn't forbidden to dabble with other supernaturals or even humans, but it caused instances like this. He hadn't felt human because of his shifter bloodline, yet there had been no way for him to know he was so much more than that.

"Maybe, but you have something to do with it too." He placed his forehead against mine. "The first time I saw you, my world shifted, and I knew it would never be the same. There's no place else I'd ever want to be, even with a scary green fae on my ass."

"I'd be lost without you." The words were simple and their meaning scarily deep. I booped him on the nose. "So one day at a time?"

"With me right by your side the entire way." He winked.

"That could be a hardship." I had to tease him. I couldn't completely melt.

"Too bad." He kissed me once more.

I moaned and deepened the kiss, enjoying his minty taste.

His hands rubbed down my sides as he responded eagerly. He groaned and pressed into me, igniting heat throughout my body.

A knock sounded on the door, followed by Roxy's scent. "Sadie? Donovan?"

"We're trying to nap," I called back as my hand slipped inside Donovan's shirt.

He chuckled sexily in my ear.

"Now that's a load of bullshit. I can smell what's going on." She knocked even harder. "We need to have a group discussion down here, so come on."

That was the equivalent of pouring a bucket of ice water all over me. "Did they find something?"

"What part of 'group discussion' did you not understand?" Roxy retorted. "Now get on down here."

"Come on." Donovan rolled off his side of the bed, frowning. "Let's go see what's going on."

"Fine." I stood, and we walked out the door.

We followed Roxy downstairs and into the living room. Everyone was waiting.

Cassius, Dawn, Titan, and Winter stood against the wall while Katherine, Lillith, Luther, Julie, Paul, and Athan sat on one of the L-shaped leather couches. Roxy, Axel, Egan, Donovan, and I sat on the other one across from them.

My attention went to the four people standing. "Did you find anything?" Maybe their time in the library had been fruitful.

"One small thing, but it's quite problematic." Cassius sighed, and his shoulders sagged. "As we expected, killing fae is very hard. With their powerful magic, it's almost impossible."

Lillith crossed her legs and leaned back in her seat. "Okay, this doesn't sound good so far."

He glared at his daughter. "I never said this would be a good conversation, dear, but facts are facts, and it's time we all knew them."

"Hard and nearly impossible." Axel winced and waved two fingers in the air. "I got mixed vibes from that sentence."

"Oh, dear God." Cassius shook his head. "And I thought Lillith was bad enough. Now we have more smart alecks."

"It makes things interesting," Dawn said warmly. It

surprised me how they acted nothing like all of the other vampires I'd encountered, and I'd met my fair share. With Tyler being the key, it made sense he would surround himself with cruel, heartless supporters he could buy and manipulate.

"Can we focus here?" Titan scowled at me. "We have enough going on without putting up with comedians."

That prick had directed that right at me. "Just know I didn't start any of the drama you're referring to." I hated alphaholes. Each day, they irritated me more than the last.

"Not sure I can agree on that." He glowered. "My mate is an emotional wreck right now."

"And you don't think Sadie is too?" Donovan spat and scooted closer to me, our sides now touching. "It's not like Winter is the only one struggling with this revelation."

"You two, stop it," Winter scolded. "We have to focus on the fae. They will be back, and any of us getting hurt is not an option."

"When you say it's hard, what do you mean exactly?" The thought of killing them, though, didn't sit well with me. They were my people, after all. "And is there a way to shut them down instead of flat out killing them?"

"Are you serious?" Titan asked, looking at me like I had two heads. "You don't want to kill them?"

"In all fairness, if we kill them, we'll only anger the rest of the fae." Roxy gestured to me like it had been my point the entire time. "So that's a good point."

You know that was not what I was getting at. I loved that girl with all my heart.

Bish, please. Roxy huffed. *Own it before Titan attacks your pretty face and Donovan and I are forced to kill him.*

Titan bared his teeth at me. "Is this amusing to you?"

"I get you're upset that I'm hurting," Winter touched

her mate's shoulder. "But you need to chill out. She's hurting too. This is a horrible situation, and she needs time to process it all."

The fact that she understood and stood up for me caught me off guard.

Titan looked like he was in pain. "But you thought she was dead ..."

"It doesn't matter." Winter sighed and scratched her head. "I lived with him for nine months, so I know what it's like."

Titan growled, not wanting to hear those words. "Don't remind me."

She pretended she hadn't heard a damn thing. "But she lived with him for eighteen years. I'm sure she endured more than I even want to consider."

"Oh yeah, she did." Roxy crossed her arms. "A weaker person would've broken and cowered, but not Sadie."

I felt like everyone's attention was on me, and I hated it. "How do we injure the fae?"

"Injuring them is our best bet." Cassius looked at me tenderly and steered the conversation back on track. "Only fae magic, ripping their hearts out, or a special knife no one knows where to find can kill them."

"A special knife?" My heart sank, and my eyes flashed to Winter's. Could that be what he had been referring to? "Is that what Tyler has?"

Something crossed her face, but I wasn't sure what. "Yeah, I'm thinking that's what he used to kill Rook."

"Who's Rook?" Axel asked.

"My biological father." I quickly filled them in on the highlights of my conversation with Winter.

"Wow, okay," Katherine said softly. "Is that why they're after you? You're a hybrid?"

"Yes, they feel the magic inside her." Winter looked at me. "And they know she's not one of them. They're trying to eliminate the threat."

I didn't even know how to use my magic, yet they viewed me as something worth eliminating. That was nice and proved people feared what they didn't understand.

"So we hide her," Donovan suggested.

"No, they can feel her power." Egan frowned. "No matter where she goes, they'll find her."

"There's nothing we can do to hide my magic?" That sounded weird, but there had to be something.

"A fae would have to hide it." Egan pursed his lips. "A powerful one. And by hiding you, they'd be going against their race."

This got better and better.

"Then we have to protect ourselves." Lillith fidgeted. "Tyler used the knife to kill Rook. How did he get it, though?"

"Tyler's family built almost all the supernatuals' houses and learned a lot of trade secrets in the process." It was stupid how easily people shared what they had with them. "From what I've gathered, the supernaturals would tell Tyler's family every object that needed extra protection. Tyler's family would then help build all the controls and secret storage places along with how to reset the passcodes for entry if something got lost."

"And people believed them." Titan shook his head in disgust. "My pack refused to use them to build our homes. We slid under the radar. Even though our pack could've gone up against them, we didn't want to kill our own kind, and they had so many supporters even back then. We just faded into the background, enjoyed the privacy, and untangled ourselves from any political agendas."

"That's one reason we've been able to hide here without issue." Winter paced in her corner. "At first, Tyler was wary of Titan, but when his pack disappeared, he didn't look for them. Mom knew their location because one of her best friends was part of this pack. We were able to escape here. Tyler had no clue where Titan and his pack landed, and Tyler won't chance finding Titan in case Titan challenges him."

"You could take him?" Athan asked as he straightened his shoulders. "Then why don't you end this mess now?"

"Because he's gotten much bigger and has more followers than before." Titan blew out a breath. "I don't stand a chance now. We don't have the backing."

"And Tyler is ruthless." We couldn't forget that. "He'd send a vampire here to kill you without a second thought."

"That's comforting." Julie laughed nervously. "What do we do?"

Egan lifted his hands. "When the fae attack, we strike hard."

Lillith's brows furrowed. "I thought the longer they stayed in our dimension, the weaker they got. They wouldn't want to draw out a fight."

"That's true." Winter nodded. "But it would take weeks for them to weaken. Their magic won't deplete within minutes unless they use a whole lot of power."

"It sounds like we need them to go all out." It was the only thing that made sense. "Make them channel all their magic somehow."

Winter sighed. "Easier said than done."

"Not if we go at them with everything we have." The problem was knowing when they'd show. I was the only one who could sense them. "Egan, dragons were originally from the fae realm. Can you tell when they appear?"

"Yes, but it's like you can." Egan rubbed the back of his neck. "It was very faint, but I picked up on it the last time you got dizzy. So between the two of us, we should have some warning even if it's small."

"Let's settle on a high-pitched whistle." Titan rubbed his chin. "Something we'll all recognize."

"The problem is, I've only shifted into wolf form once." Donovan sheepishly glanced at Luther. "And I stumbled a little, and I don't know how to fight in that form."

"Same here," Axel added.

Titan focused on the two boys. "We'll train you. We all could stand it. When they come back, we need to go all in. Every hand will be critical."

Those words turned cold inside me. It sounded like he was hinting at killing them. I didn't know or trust the man, not yet. But there was no way in hell I'd let him hurt the fae. I didn't care what I had to do to stop him.

CHAPTER FOURTEEN

Nervous energy buzzed around the room as everyone in the mansion sat at the large rectangular breakfast table. Cassius sat at one end, sipping blood from a glass, with Egan directly across from him. Dawn and Paul sat next to the older man and across from each other with Julie beside her husband.

The four younger vampires sat on the bar stools since there weren't enough seats at the table. .

"How does it feel to sit at the kids' table?" Roxy asked and took a large bite of her eggs. She winked at Dawn, who sat right next to her.

"You can kiss my ass." Lillith turned in her seat and glared at the shifter. "Axel, get your mate in line before I hurt her."

"Hey now." Axel glanced across the table at Donovan and back at Roxy, who he happened to be sitting right beside. "I couldn't control her even if I wanted to."

"Damn straight." Roxy pointed at me. "Even her dad couldn't get me to behave."

She was right. Even though he'd made it clear he didn't

approve, she stayed my friend. It infuriated him.

Donovan stiffened beside me. "He isn't her dad."

I hadn't thought twice about it until he'd pointed it out. He was protecting me, knowing I was still struggling with it. The fact that Donovan and Egan sat on either side of me spoke volumes. They protected the ones they cared about.

"Oh, you're right." She grimaced and clenched her teeth. "I'm sorry, girl."

"No, it's fine." Them feeling like they had to watch what they said around me would only make things worse. I needed them to treat me like they normally did. "It's going to take time for us to adjust." I forced myself to take a bite of food so she would know she hadn't upset me.

"Why are we all up and eating breakfast together this morning?" Egan asked, clearly thinking the same thing as me and diverting the conversation away from my parentage.

I'd found it odd when Lillith had asked us to join them for breakfast. I'd quickly packed a bag with extra clothes for the shifters before coming down. I hadn't pushed since we needed to get moving on the day. Our priority was to get our surroundings down in animal form.

"Titan called me this morning and suggested we should come over." Cassius avoided my gaze. "I told him it was a good idea."

"Why?" The last thing I wanted was to go there and face not only Winter but potentially my grandparents. "We all talked yesterday."

"First off, let's figure out how to get the fae to use up their magic," Cassius said sternly, not liking being challenged. "And two, if his pack is going to fight beside us, it'd be nice if you got to know them."

Ugh, he had a point. Even Tyler knew to play nice with his allies. "Fine." My appetite vanished.

If you don't want to go ... Donovan started, acting as the considerate mate he naturally was.

No, he's right. I wanted to pout, but that would make everything ten times worse. *They're going to fight beside us.* Hell, they already had twice now. *It's only right that we spend time with them.*

Maybe you could stay back?

Nope. I was the alpha of our little pack, and they were facing a battle against the fae because of me. *It's only right that I go, but thank you.* I squeezed his leg lovingly.

Axel chewed the rest of his pancake and licked the syrup off his lips. "What do you think we should expect?"

"Well, I'll know whether Titan is game or not. You two," Egan said, pointing at Donovan and Axel, "need to shift again and bond with your wolves."

"We're supposed to be there in twenty minutes." Katherine tapped her phone. "Are you all about done?"

"Talk about springing it on us." Roxy lifted an eyebrow. "On behalf of my sister from another mister, I'm not thrilled about this."

"Exactly why we waited." Lillith stuck her tongue out at her. "We didn't want to hear you whine and complain the whole time."

"You two behave." Dawn pointed a finger at Lillith. "You two are acting up while Sadie is taking it in stride."

I wasn't sure I would consider it in stride. My half-eaten plate of food mocked me. I should have eaten more, but my stomach wouldn't allow it. "I'm ready whenever you are."

Everyone else had cleaned their plates, which further frayed my nerves.

Donovan motioned to my plate. "Are you sure you don't want to eat more?"

"No, I'm good, and Katherine is right. We're supposed

to meet them soon." I stood, grabbed the duffle bag that contained a change of clothes for us, and headed to the sink. "We don't have much time. We should get going."

The group followed suit with the shifters putting their plates in the sink and the vampires rinsed their glasses.

I was the first one out the door, needing a small reprieve from Egan's and Donovan's watchful gazes. Their attention was daunting. Even though I could be honest with Donovan, I needed to find the strength within me. He could be my rock, but I had to stand on my own.

Roxy linked with me. *Wait up.*

I slowed but didn't stop. I wanted to maintain some distance.

She caught up within seconds and walked next to me. *How are you doing?* she asked.

I'm fine. Maybe that wasn't the complete truth, but we needed our heads in the game. I didn't need to wallow or get all emotional. It was hard enough heading straight into Titan's pack.

She pursed her lips but stopped her line of questioning.

We walked through the woods quickly. We moved faster and faster until the trees flew past us as we ran. That was the nice thing about all of us being supernaturals. We could move faster than a human and didn't have to worry about them seeing us.

From what Lillith and Katherine had told us, the closest human neighborhood was over thirty miles away.

Normally, I'd enjoy being out here like this. We allowed our wolves to peek through. I'd have shifted if we hadn't been meeting up with Titan. But I needed to stay human to communicate with the other pack. However, my wolf was getting restless. It'd been way too long since I'd let her out.

My skin crawled the deeper we got into the woods. The

fae seemed to appear without much notice. I could only hope they wouldn't cloak themselves from me, but from what I'd gathered, they refused to. They wanted to make sure we knew they were coming.

"Everything okay up there?" Athan called from the back.

He wasn't as quiet as Luther, but still not loud. The same could be said about Katherine's parents. But he liked feeling included when possible. "Yeah, I don't sense them." I glanced over my shoulder at Egan, Donovan, and Axel directly behind us. "Do you, Egan?"

"No, I don't." He scanned the area, on high alert. "But we still need to be careful."

I focused forward again. The air was chilly, and the leaves were turning various shades of reds and oranges. Fall was here and in full effect. This was my least favorite time of year. Everything was dying, which meant the holidays would be here soon.

Thanksgiving and Christmas were isolating and lonely. Most of the time, Dad had run off, not wanting to be near me. I'd wound up spending the holidays at Roxy's house. Even though they were kind and accepting, they hated my father. They'd never said those words to me, but it was clear they'd wished to spend the holidays without me.

Luckily, we were getting to Titan's pack without any issues. I didn't know why I'd expected to run into the fae first thing. Last time, a few days had passed between attacks.

When the trees thinned, my legs almost collapsed with relief when I saw Winter and Titan standing outside with forty men.

At least I didn't have to worry about going inside and running into my grandparents right away. Even though shifters aged slowly, I'd bet money that Winter refused to let them fight.

"Hey." Winter smiled at me but didn't move closer.

Maybe she'd meant it yesterday when she'd said she'd respect my wishes. "Hi."

Titan nodded at me and launched straight into business. "These are our strongest fighters. The others aren't fit for this kind of battle."

A tall, thick fighter's eyes widened. "Whoa, is that a dragon?" He appeared to be in his twenties, and his long black hair was pulled into a low ponytail.

"Yes, I am." Egan sounded amused. "And you are?"

"Torak." He pointed to Titan. "He's my dad, so I guess that means ..." His eyes landed on me. "... you're my sister."

My heart stilled. I'd always wanted a sibling growing up, and I hadn't even considered the possibility that I might have one. I didn't know how to respond.

"Step-sister," Winter clarified.

"Eh, same difference." He grinned, and it surprised me that he came off as a nice guy. "And the broody one must be your mate." His dark green eyes locked on Donovan and stopped on Axel. "Dude, you smell so familiar."

"What?" Axel's brows furrowed. "I'm not sure what that means."

I glanced at Winter, who looked everywhere but at me.

"Nothing worth discussing right now," Titan said forcefully.

"Uh ..." Torak laughed nervously. "Yeah."

A scent could be tied to a family. If Torak recognized Axel's scent, that could be huge. Could they know who Axel's family was? Now wasn't the time to ask and get his hopes up, but if Winter thought we wouldn't be talking about this, she'd find out otherwise.

"We thought it would be wise if we all hung out in animal form together," Titan said. "That way, our animals can get to know each other, and you and Egan can alert us if the fae show up."

"That sounds like a good plan." Even though I was scared, we had to do this. "But a few of us need to stay in human form so we can talk." I normally would shift with them, but I wanted to be able to communicate with Egan, Cassius, and Titan. If yesterday's conversation was any indicator, I wanted to make it clear that killing any fae wasn't an option.

"Yeah, that's a smart idea." Titan gestured to the vamps. "Maybe we could hang back and strategize."

"Then, let's get to shifting." Torak headed over to the tree line with the pack following him. Axel and Roxy headed to their own section.

Are you sure I shouldn't stay human too? Donovan took my hand and turned me toward him. *I don't mind.*

No, you can protect yourself better by getting familiar with your wolf. I stood on my tiptoes and pressed my lips to his. *I'll be right there with you.*

"Maybe you can get the wolves to train you." Cassius glanced at the younger vampires. "It would be good for you to see how they move and maybe even brawl with them. The more we can get in sync with one another, the better."

"Sounds like fun." Athan clapped his hands. "I've never fought a wolf before."

"Remember to play fight." Julie pointed at him. "There will be no injuries."

"Fine," Luther whined, but the happiness in his eyes shone through. "We'll behave."

The wolves soon emerged from where they'd all changed and ran in our direction. The vampires and Egan took off after them, leaving Winter, Cassius, Titan, and me behind.

We walked quickly to catch up to them.

"Did you all brainstorm any more last night?" I asked, jumping straight to the point. If any decisions had been made without me, I wanted to know sooner rather than later. Obviously, he and Cassius had talked this morning.

"As of now, I don't see how any of our plans can change." Titan's shoulders tightened. "We don't know how many fae will show up next time, and we need to be prepared. Fortunately, I haven't used all my fighters, so they don't know our exact numbers, but I've used most. We'll need to do whatever it takes to survive."

"No, we aren't killing them." Did he not know how bad that would make this? "That's not an option. We have to be peaceful."

"Now, listen here." Titan took a menacing step in my direction. "You're young and emotional. You're not the one who gets to make these decisions."

"I agree with her," Cassius cut in, coming to my aid. "It would cause a huge war that we can't win. There has to be another option."

I hadn't expected the older vampire to agree with me.

"Which would be what?" he spat.

"Iron." I'd stayed up researching fae lore last night and stumbled upon a credible website. "It's a fae weakness and how we can absorb their magic. I tested it last night, and the iron drained me. When they shoot their magic at us, the iron should drain their magic too. It's a way we can get them to channel their magic at us."

Winter jerked her head in my direction. "How did you learn this?"

"I used the world wide web to my advantage." I lifted my fingers. "And found something."

"But there's no way to verify it—" Titan started, but Winter cut him off.

"Yes, there is." A proud look filled her face. "So you tested it."

Titan's forehead lined. "How is that possible?"

"The bed I'm sleeping in has iron bars on it." I'd gotten excited with that little revelation last night. "So I touched it. I immediately felt drained and fell asleep."

"But how is that going to help us?" Cassius tilted his head. "I guess we could take the metal off the bed and cut it."

"No, we have something even easier than that." Titan stopped walking and looked mildly impressed. "A pack member owns a scrap metal business. It's where the whole city drops their stuff off. We should have plenty."

"Do we need to head over there?" The sooner we got the iron, the safer we'd be.

"I'll get some of the guys to go now."

A few seconds after he'd said that, five wolves ran past us back to the pack.

"It should only take them a couple of hours to get things settled," Winter said with relief. "I've been so worried, but maybe we'll be okay."

"By the time we're done running"—Titan motioned toward the others—"they should be back. We can eat dinner and get everything organized."

"Sounds good." Cassius nodded. "But we'll need blood."

"We've got you covered," Titan reassured him.

What we'd agreed to do finally set in. In just a few hours, there would be no getting around meeting my grandparents, and I wasn't sure I was ready.

CHAPTER FIFTEEN

Running around in wolf form was so freeing. Despite our paranoia that the fae would show up any second, our group got to know each other and roughhoused.

Also, my wolf being free made a huge difference. She'd felt caged and trapped so much recently that it was a wonder I hadn't come completely unhinged.

This is really nice. Donovan linked with me as he jumped on me. I tumbled over and landed on my back. He playfully nipped at my leg, which was sticking straight up. *And I didn't try to attack a vampire, so that's a huge win!*

Good job. We'd been in animal form for over three hours, and it had been touch and go for him and Axel at first, but they'd settled into their wolves within minutes.

The vampires were brave enough to allow the new wolves to fight with them, and Egan had a huge smile on his face as he fought hard against Torak. They'd developed a quick friendship.

It proved what I'd always suspected: Donovan and Axel needed significant time in their animal forms without any threats around. I could feel their contentedness and, dare I say, happiness.

I rolled to my side, jumped onto his back, and gently bit into his neck. My wolf wanted to claim him, and I had to clamp her down. There were a ton of people around, and it was not the right time. But he was finally getting to a point where we could take the next step in our relationship.

Hey, you, he growled and stood on his hind legs, making me fall back onto all fours. He hunkered over me, his teeth right at my neck.

He must have felt the same way as I did.

Axel charged over and steamrolled Donovan into a tree, saving us from a very uncomfortable situation.

Roxy trotted over and sat next to me. We watched our mates together. *It's like the calm before the storm.*

Don't remind me. I wanted to enjoy the moment and not worry about the future. *Let's not dampen the day.*

Fate must have heard and decided to take matters into her own hands because Titan and Winter stepped into the small clearing. They'd gone back to the pack to prepare for the iron materials and insisted we all hang out together.

"Hey, the iron is here," Titan said as he motioned for us to follow him. "It'd be nice to have all-hands-on-deck to unload it."

Winter's face softened as she took in our group. We'd all gotten along, and we'd run around the woods a couple of times. We had gained our bearings, which would come in handy and give us a leg up on the fae.

Let's get moving. We needed to prepare before the fae popped up again.

Yes, ma'am, Roxy teased as she raced me toward the area we'd all changed in.

I went a little deeper into the woods, putting some

distance between me and the other male shifters. I heard Donovan following close behind me. The two of us changed back into our human forms, and it took every ounce of self-control I had not to run over and lick his naked body. The tribal tattoo on his shoulder pulled my attention in the glistening sun. It was funny that I hadn't paid attention to it since the first day I'd seen him. Usually, I was focused on his stomach, lips, or elsewhere, but the tattoo made him over-the-top sexy.

"See something you like?" He smirked, but his eyes were scanning me hungrily too.

"Nope." A grin spread across my face. "Not at all." The stench of the lie filled the air.

Donovan's nose wrinkled in disgust, and he pulled on his shirt. *Can you please not make those kinds of smells while we're naked and checking each other out?*

Hey, it's your fault. I laughed so hard my sides hurt. *I had to do something to keep you from devouring me.*

Wait until tonight. He pulled on his pants, but the threat in his eyes was clear. *Not even that smell will keep me away.*

My body warmed at the promise. *You know, I hate liars.*

Then I can't disappoint. He watched as I quickly dressed.

Soon, we were stepping out to join the others. That was when it hit me. Yes, I wanted to deal with the iron, but that would come at the price of meeting my grandparents. *Do you think I might get away with not having to meet my grandparents?*

If you don't want to, I'll make sure it doesn't happen. Donovan took my hand. *I won't allow you to be pressured into anything you aren't ready for.*

He knew exactly what was making me nervous without

me having to spill my guts; he had a way of making me fall in love with him all over again. But I'd realized something today while running with everyone. *I think I need to. It could be my only chance to meet them.*

Sadie, Roxy chastised, interrupting our conversation. *You are not going to die. If you do, I'll kill you myself.*

Babe, you do realize that's not actually possible. Axel stepped out of the woods and joined us. *She'd be dead. You wouldn't be able to kill her.*

Shut it. Roxy glared at him. *You get the point.*

"Are you two bickering again?" Lillith walked over, her pale skin slightly pink from being in the sun all day. "You've got that miserable but infatuated look going on."

All of the vampires had the sun-kissed glow. If it hadn't been for their overly sweet smell, they actually could have passed as real humans.

"Leave them alone." Katherine snorted. "Bickering is their foreplay. You should know this by now."

"Katherine." She was usually the better-mannered of the two. "You're turning into Lillith."

She shrugged.

"We don't need another one," Egan retorted as he joined our small group. "We have enough smart-asses to last us a lifetime.

"For the record, I can't help it." Roxy lifted her chin. "I have red hair. It's in my blood, and being called a smart-ass is not necessarily an insult."

"I'm sorry, man," Donovan said and smacked Axel in the arm. "But you've always enjoyed a good argument, so maybe you've met your match."

It was strange, but for the first time ever, my life felt complete. If it wasn't for the angry fae breathing down our necks and Tyler searching for me, it would've been the happiest I'd ever been.

The group headed toward the pack homes, and my heart rate increased. I wasn't sure what to expect when my grandparents saw me.

Winter stopped walking. When Donovan and I caught up, she touched my arm. "Did you have a good day today?"

"Actually, yeah." There was no reason to lie. Hell, she'd have known if I did. "The guys were fun to run with, and I was surprised at how strong they all are. We have a fighting chance against the fae."

"That's one reason Tyler was so nervous about Titan." She dropped her hand but kept pace with us. "They are really strong here."

"You'd think he'd keep an eye out for Titan around here to see where he wound up settling." It seemed like something Tyler would do. "I mean ... 'keep your enemies close' is kind of his motto."

"I'm sure he's tried." Egan glanced over his shoulder at us. "He'd want to keep tabs on them."

"He has no clue where Titan's pack moved." She waved her hands around the woods. "They've always lived in the Smoky Mountains but in a town two hours from here. That was where we met. When we realized we were fated mates, I told him everything. We picked up and moved here. Cassius actually took us in at the mansion while the houses were being built."

That didn't surprise me. Cassius seemed like a caring vampire. It spoke volumes that he hadn't kicked our sorry asses out.

"The homes are simple but nice inside," she explained as the clearing that led to their homes came into view. Just like the other day, we saw the simple two-story log cabins. There were at least one hundred of them with two large houses at the center. They were all well maintained and sturdy. "They do what we need them to, and the pack built them themselves so no one outside us would know the location."

Roxy caught up to us. "The wood cabins go perfectly with this area, so it's not like anything would appear out of sorts either."

"Exactly." Winter nodded. "The more basic they are, the less we stand out. We want to blend in."

As we stepped into the clearing, the smell of meat cooking filled my nose, and my stomach gurgled loudly. After running for three hours straight, I was famished, and it'd been a while since I'd had a good steak. "That smells delicious."

"Clearly." Roxy gestured to my stomach. "We all heard that."

"I'm with her on that one." Egan scanned the area. "It's been a while since I was this hungry."

"Wait, you eat like a pig normally." Roxy frowned. "You better save some for the rest of us. It isn't all yours."

"Before anyone gets to eat," Titan said, pointing to a huge, red F250 truck with a bed full of iron, "let's unload that and get it sorted. Torak, you and the others go help finish up cooking and get everything laid out."

"But Dad ..." Torak pouted.

"No buts." Titan used his alpha voice. "Go now. The vampires, dragon, and Sadie's pack will be plenty."

"Fine." The young man turned and waved the wolves toward a bigger building. Smoke billowed from behind it. "Let's go before the girls get hangry."

"Oh, and make sure the vamps have plenty of blood," Titan called after the retreating figures.

Torak lifted a thumb in the air.

"Let's get this going." Cassius clapped his hands and headed over to the bed. "I guess we should divvy them up by size."

"No, we're going to have someone melt it into shields." Titan gestured to a wolf about five yards over who was setting up in a large open area between several houses. He had a black box on the ground with wires coming out the top. "He's got a forge that will melt the iron, and we can go from there. We just need help carrying the stuff over."

"Well, okay then." Egan picked up a long pole. His face tensed, and he dropped it back down in the bed. "Holy shit. That was draining me." His eyes latched on to mine. "It must be because I have diluted fae blood in my body."

"Crap." I remembered feeling stripped and raw. "So you can't help either."

"That's fine." Donovan walked over to Egan and patted his back. "We've got it."

The vampires, my pack, Winter, and Titan carried the materials over to the man. Egan and I stood on the sidelines, watching.

"I feel worthless," he grumbled and crossed his arms. "I should be helping them."

"And so should I." I didn't like it either. "But that leaves a very interesting question."

He leaned toward me. "What's that?"

I lowered my voice so only the dragon could hear. "We can't use the iron to protect ourselves." I was stating the obvious, but the others hadn't considered it yet. If they had, Donovan would have pitched a fit.

"You're right." Egan nodded. "I promise nothing will happen to you."

Yeah, that hadn't quite gone the way I'd expected it.

"No, you need to protect your own ass. You don't need to worry about me."

"Sadie." Egan tilted his head and glared at me. "You're one of my best friends. Of course I'll do everything possible to save you."

And that was what it all boiled down to. Egan was a great guy and an all-around good friend. "Just promise me if something happens, you'll make sure they all stay safe." I glanced at my friends out of the corner of my eye. "That you'll force Donovan to move on and find someone who will make him happy."

"You're talking as if you know you're going to die." Egan's forehead lined with worry, and he turned toward me. "You aren't planning something, right?"

"No," I said way too loudly. I, at least, didn't think I'd do anything stupid. I didn't have some sort of complex where I wanted to purposely inflict pain on myself. "Why would you say something like that?"

"Because people say things like that before they make some not-so-smart decisions," Egan said slowly ... almost gently. "You're not going to be not smart, right?"

"Egan, is that your way of asking if I'm going to do something stupid?" Even when he insulted a friend, he did it like a gentleman.

"Essentially." He licked his lips and rubbed his chin. "If so, I might need to talk with the others."

Dear God. Now I wish I hadn't brought anything up. "No conversation is needed." I placed a hand on my heart. "I promise, nothing stupid will happen." At the end of the day, I wanted all of us to survive and live long and happy lives.

Not wanting him to grill me any longer, I saw some gloves sitting near the furnace. I raced over and grabbed them before jumping on the truck bed. I slipped the gloves on as protection to grab an iron post. I wasn't sure if it would work, and I stiffened as I reached for the iron. I closed my eyes and took hold, waiting for it to drain me.

"Sadie, what are you doing?" Donovan yelled.

When nothing happened, I opened my eyes and grinned. "Helping." I got to the edge of the bed and jumped to the ground. "If I use the gloves, I'm good." I glanced at Egan. "So we only need a thick barrier like these."

"That makes sense." Egan smiled with relief. "Even if we have to use a shirt, I'm down."

Two sets of footsteps headed in our direction, and I heard someone take a large gasp of air. "Oh, my God."

I tensed, and my eyes landed on two older shifters.

CHAPTER SIXTEEN

Winter looked identical to the older lady staring at me. The only difference was the wrinkles around her eyes and the gray highlights in her light blonde hair. She even had her hair pulled back in a ponytail as Winter did. She was taller than me by two inches, which wasn't surprising. I was more of a petite shifter.

The older man beside her was striking. He had all-gray hair except for a spatter of brown throughout. He towered over the lady, but his warm topaz eyes made him seem less intimidating.

"Mom," Winter warned, giving her a stern look. "We talked about this."

"No, you talked." The older lady ran over to me and pulled me into a strong hug. "I pretended to listen."

With all of the warmth and comfort it provided, her embrace caught me off guard. Next to Donovan, I'd never felt so safe. Even with the iron pole between us, it didn't feel awkward. My instinct to drop the iron and return the hug almost overwhelmed me, but that would have injured her and my feet.

The older man chuckled. "Darlin', she's holding on to something. You ought to let her go."

"Oh, yeah." She released her hold as her light blue eyes filled with tears. "It's just ... I never thought I'd see you again. Yet, here you are."

Donovan slowly walked closer to me, letting me know he was there. He gave us a wide enough berth, not impeding on the moment.

I placed the iron down, and then removed and dropped the gloves, feeling no desire to step away. It was odd. I didn't feel any resistance or hesitation with her. "I thought I'd never meet you." I wanted to get to know her. It alarmed me.

"You saw plenty enough of me the week you were born." She patted my arm. "Not even that deadbeat alpha could keep me away."

"He tried?" It shouldn't have surprised me. He was the controlling type. Having them around would have lessened his influence over Winter and me. "I guess that's not shocking."

"That day we thought you died ..."

"Mom, now isn't the time or place." Winter gestured to our group of people. "We're unloading the iron."

The older lady looked at me. "Then why don't you come take a short walk with Feng and me. I'm sure they have plenty of hands to help them."

"Uh ... okay." I couldn't say no. "If that's okay with all of you?" I glanced at our group, not wanting to leave them shorthanded.

"Yeah, we're good." Donovan smiled at me encouragingly. "Take all the time you need." *Just don't go too far since the fae could show up at any time.*

Of course. His support meant so much to me. *I won't be gone long.*

"Hey, I get to go too, right?" Roxy pouted and headed over to the older lady. "I'm Roxy, her best friend. Well, more like a sister."

"I figured that was you with that red hair." The older lady laughed. "I was there the day you were born. Your red hair was the prettiest thing I'd seen before Sadie here was born." She hugged my best friend too. "And my name is Sherry, but if what you say is true, I guess Grams is in order."

"All I heard was that I'm joining you three." She motioned to Feng, her, and then me.

"Nope, not happening." Lillith hurried over and grabbed Roxy by the arm. "You're just trying to get out of work. You get to help. Give her a second with them."

Roxy rolled her eyes and begrudgingly grabbed more iron. "So not fair."

"Come on." Sherry chuckled as the three of us took off toward the woods.

We walked in silence until we were far enough away that the others couldn't hear us.

Sherry stared at me, examining my face. "Your hair didn't change one bit."

I felt like I was under a microscope. I tried not to flinch, but it reminded me of Tyler and how he'd examine me before an event to ensure I looked the part.

"You're freaking her out." Feng took his wife's hand and pulled her a few steps away from me. "You're staring at her like she's a statue."

"It's just ..." She sniffled. "I'm afraid she'll disappear."

"I'm not going anywhere." Even if I'd wanted to, that wasn't an option. I was safest here. The last thing I needed was for Tyler and the fae to attack me at the same time. "But it does put your pack at a bigger risk because of the fae."

"You're worth it." Sherry patted her chest. "Don't think for a second you aren't."

"Winter told us you were at a university," Feng said, taking control of the conversation. "What were you going to school for?"

"Undecided." I hadn't thought very far ahead. "I just wanted to get away from Tyler." As soon as the words had left my mouth, I wished I could take them back. It told them way more than I'd meant to.

"To think you were alone with him for eighteen years." Sherry shook her head and wrinkled her nose. "You must be a very strong woman to have survived it."

"It's not like I had a choice." I sounded more bitter than I intended, but sometimes, the truth wasn't all sunshine. "I thought he was my father and my mother was dead."

"Still, he didn't break you." Feng shook a finger at me. "That means a lot. Winter struggled those nine months with him."

"She seems pretty strong." I had a hard time believing that. "I'm sure she managed better than you imagined."

"Oh, sweet girl, she didn't." Sherry rubbed a hand down her face. "I wasn't sure she would make it through the pregnancy."

She had to be exaggerating. "What do you mean?" I'd seen how much hell she gave Titan.

"Well, your father …" Feng paused and lifted a finger. "Your real father became her best friend and confidant. She'd never been that close to someone before."

"We warned her," Sherry interjected. "The fae can be very alluring and charming when they want to be. That's what makes them dangerous like a vampire. But with them, it's worse because they're much more powerful."

"But like any young, foolish, headstrong girl," Feng continued, "she didn't listen."

I loved how they told the story together. They had to be fated mates who'd been together a long time. It was how I pictured Donovan and me long into the future—if we ever made it that far. "I know how it ended, with Rook dead and all."

"Yes, but your mother was racked with guilt." Sherry's eyes filled with pain. "She blamed herself for everything. If it hadn't been for you, I don't think she would've made it nine months, but she loved you before she even felt your first kick. It gave her time to plan her escape ... to save you."

I almost lost it at the absurdity of that statement. "That didn't go over well, now, did it?"

"It's easy to judge others when you aren't the one having to make decisions." Feng lifted a brow with disapproval. "Who knows what you would've done. Hindsight is always twenty-twenty."

Wow, his disappointment hurt. How had that happened so fast? "You're right, but growing up with no mother and an overly critical father ... it wasn't easy."

"And her waking up each day, trying to live a somewhat fulfilling life while blaming herself for Rook's death and her daughter's ..." Sherry wrapped an arm around my shoulders and pulled me near. "Try that for a change. She thought Tyler killed you because he'd found out you weren't his."

Dammit, they were softening me toward her. "Is that why you wanted to come out here and talk?" I'd hoped they had wanted to get to know me. Maybe it was all about Winter.

"Of course not." Feng strolled to my other side. "We

wanted some alone time with you. We have a lot of catching up to do, but you need to see things from Winter's perspective. You're all she ever talks about, and you not wanting to get close to her is killing her."

"Okay." They were making me feel bad. I had a feeling that was the point. "I get it. I'll try to keep more of an open mind."

"That's all we're asking." Sherry placed a hand on my arm. "I knew you would be a smart, sensitive woman."

Tyler had gone on and on about how women weren't good leaders for that reason alone. Of course, when there was a woman he wanted to get close to, he kept those negative thoughts to himself. "Doesn't that make me weak?"

"No, that makes the strongest women more dangerous." Feng forced a shiver. "That means you can gain allies and never underestimate the underdog."

I'd never heard anyone put it quite like that. "Are you saying Grams here wears the pants in the relationship?"

"Damn straight she does." Feng looked lovingly at his wife. "She keeps my ass in line."

"Somebody has to." She lifted her head and looked at me. "This man would walk around naked without me. As soon as he gets in the house, his clothes come off. He's embarrassed everyone here at least once with his nudist tendencies."

"We're shifters. We're supposed to embrace it." He gestured at me. "Tell her."

I tried keeping a straight face while looking at the man who could be very intimidating if he wanted. "I've got to say I never want to see you naked." That was something I would never get out of my head.

"See." Sherry sounded so proud. "She's on my side."

Hey. Donovan linked with me. *We're done unloading, and the food's almost ready. We're here waiting on you three.*

On it. I'd enjoyed my alone time with those two, but I was ready to get back to the others. "They want us back."

"Yeah, Winter just linked with us," Feng said as we all turned around. "Are you ready to head back?"

"I'm starving, so getting closer to steak sounds really great to me." My stomach rumbled again, driving the point home. "See."

"Yup, we sure do." Sherry laughed.

I envied Sherry's carefree attitude.

We spent the next little bit in silence until I realized there was one more thing I wanted to address before we got back. "Hey, can I ask one more question?"

"You're free to ask us anything." Sherry looped her arm through mine. "Just make sure you want the real answer."

Now that was sound advice. "So Torak ... I mean, Titan has a son, and she had me. Why didn't they..." I didn't even know how to finish that sentence.

"Titan had a chosen mate, but she died giving birth to Torak." A frown marred her face. "He raised that sweet boy alone until Winter stumbled here. She fought the bond for a while, but fate always wins. She never wanted to have another child."

"She said no one could ever replace you." Feng mashed his lips into a line. "And we all respected that decision."

I was the reason she didn't have children with Titan. I didn't know why, but I felt guilty. It wasn't like I'd forced her into that decision, but maybe she loved me more than I realized. Now I wasn't sure what my next steps should be.

"It's okay to take your time." Sherry patted my arm. "We just wanted a chance to talk to you and tell you the full story that I don't even think Winter realizes, but we are here to support you too. You've had a lot thrown your way, and it's not something we will ever take for granted."

What would my life have been like with these amazing, supportive people in it from the very beginning? It seemed cruel that I hadn't gotten to know them until now.

We stepped back into the clearing and found the group waiting on us. We all headed to dinner together.

DONOVAN OPENED the door to our bedroom, and we stumbled inside.

"That was a fun night." He snagged my hand and pulled me toward the bed. "Your grandparents are crazy."

"They are." They'd had the table laughing all night, and the usual awkwardness around Titan and Winter hadn't been there. "In the best way possible."

"Hey, I'm not complaining." A huge smile filled his face. "They were calling me grandson by the end of the night."

"You are my fated mate." I stared into his eyes, loving to see the happiness in them. It'd been a while. "So you're their grandson too."

"I should've known they'd be amazing." He lowered his lips to mine. "Only truly great people could have made someone amazing like you."

I broke into a peal of laughter and moved my head out of the way, dodging his kiss. I wasn't trying to be an ass, but I couldn't hold it back.

"What the hell?" he said gruffly. "What was that for?"

"That might have been the cheesiest thing you've ever said." It was a good thing he was damn hot or things could've gone south between us with that line.

"Cheesy." He huffed and grabbed me, pulling me back into his arms. He pressed his lips to mine, cutting off my laughter.

I closed my eyes and returned his kiss.

Is that cheesy? he growled and deepened the kiss.

My brain could barely think coherently. *Nope, not at all.*

He took my waist and hoisted me up against him.

I wrapped my legs around his waist and rubbed against him, needing friction. The need slammed into me like never before. My wolf was desperate for him.

His breathing grew ragged as he lowered me onto the bed. He snatched my hands and kept them firmly in place by my head. He then tore his lips from mine and kissed down my neck, nibbling and driving me damn near insane.

I needed him, and my wolf surged forward, wanting to claim him.

Within a second, his teeth nipped at my neck, desperate for the same thing.

Can I? he rasped in my mind and pulled back, scanning my face. He fought for control, not wanting his wolf to take over until he got permission.

I raised my head so I could look him in the eye. I wanted him to know I felt the exact same way. *Yes, please.*

Thank God. He lowered his face to my neck and slipped his hand inside my jeans.

I heard his mouth open and felt his breath on my neck. My heart pounded, waiting for this to finally happen.

Then the room began to spin, and I grew dizzy. My head lobbed to the side.

They were here.

CHAPTER SEVENTEEN

Donovan removed his hands from my pants and lifted himself onto his elbow. "What's wrong?"

I hated to ruin our moment, but it wasn't like I could control this. My stomach roiled, and the room spun faster. *The fae. They're here.*

He tensed and scanned the room. *What do you mean, here?*

It wasn't an exact science. *Hell if I know.* From what I'd gathered, I could feel it when they transported nearby. I couldn't pinpoint their location. *Roxy. Axel. We have a problem.*

Axel sounded annoyed. *Dude, do you need another condom? You need to buy in bulk.*

Apparently, Roxy and Axel were in the middle of something themselves. Hopefully, we'd stopped them before they'd gotten too far along.

No, dipshit, Donovan growled. *It's not time for jokes. The fae are here.*

Shit. Roxy linked. *What do we do?*

The only thing we could. *Get ready to fight.* All the iron

was over at Titan's. This wasn't ideal. *I'll get Egan and the others while you three get it together.* I forced myself to sit up and blinked to focus my eyes. Last time, I'd pushed through it, so there had to be a way this time too.

I stepped toward the door, but Donovan grabbed my arm, stopping me. He said, "Let me get Cassius and the others. You get Egan. Baby steps until you get your bearings again."

It pissed me off that I had to be slow and steady, but he was right. Adrenaline rushed inside me, clearing whatever fog the fae had caused. "We'll meet you in the kitchen." For all I knew, the fae could attack the house at any moment.

He opened the door and took off toward the stairs.

In an effort to keep from pushing myself yet, I walked slowly to Egan's bedroom and pounded on the door. "Egan."

It opened immediately.

Egan's pupils were in slits, his dragon already surfaced. "I felt it too. There have to be a ton of them." He breathed hard, and smoke trickled out his nostrils.

That I agreed with. "We're supposed to meet the others in the kitchen." I'd bet the fae were out in the woods behind the house. That seemed to be where they stayed. The front side was closer to a road and other humans. Fae wanted to keep their existence a complete secret. They didn't allow anyone else to enter their realm.

The door across the hall opened, and Axel and Roxy joined me in the hallway.

Roxy's forehead was lined with worry. "Are we sure it's them?"

That question annoyed the shit out of me. "I'm dizzy just like all the other times, and Egan felt it more strongly than normal too, so that's a hard yes."

"We don't need to take out our frustration on each

other." Egan touched my shoulder. "Let's head down and channel it on them."

He had a point. "Come on." I hurried to the stairs, and my vision seemed clearer. Don't get me wrong, my head was still fuzzy, proving they were still here, but I could focus beyond that.

The three followed close behind, and as we passed the den, the sound of heavy footsteps coming in our direction comforted me. At least, we were all together before they attacked.

Cassius and Donovan came into view with the rest following closely behind.

The older vampire had a cell phone to his ear, and his usually pale face was flushed.

"Titan, I don't know where they are. All we know is they're here."

There was a pause while he listened to Titan's reply.

Donovan headed over to me and cupped my face. "Are you doing any better?"

"Yeah." I still wasn't back at my full, normal self, but I was better than I'd been minutes ago. "I think there are a lot here."

"Can they come into the house?" Axel asked as he surveyed the area. "Or do they have to be invited in?"

"They aren't vampires." Lillith rolled her eyes. "Nothing's holding them back."

That was the nice thing about the dorms: they weren't tied to an individual resident but rather rolling dwellers. Vampires didn't have to be invited in just like regular public places.

Cassius hung up the phone. "They want us to meet them at least halfway. The closer we can get to their pack, the better since that's where all the iron is."

"We should've brought some back with us." I hated that we hadn't considered the possibility. We'd all had a good time earlier tonight and let our guard down. "But if we're heading that way, we need to move. The more time we give them to set up a perimeter, the harder it'll be to get past them."

"Let's go shift into our wolves." Donovan rubbed his face. "We need to be in our strongest form from the start."

"Then how are you going to hold iron?" I agreed with him, but if we could get to the metal, it'd do us more good. "I think we push ourselves in human form and get there as quickly as possible."

"She has a point," Roxy agreed. "We already know they can kick our asses in animal form. Do we need a repeat performance?"

"I'll fly high and search for a path around the fae." Egan pulled off his shirt. "And if I can distract them, I will. If I roar three times, that means to run hard and fast because they're focused on me."

"Tired of ripping all of your shirts from your body?" Lillith retorted. "I bet you don't have many left."

"Lillith," Dawn chastised. "The man is helping us, and you're going to insult him like that?"

"Don't worry." Katherine patted the woman's arm. "He's used to it."

"Not helping." Lillith play-scowled at her best friend. "Now I'm going to hear about it even more."

"We need to take this seriously." Paul hurried into the kitchen. "Everybody move."

Egan pushed forward and opened the back door. As soon as he stepped outside, he dropped his pants and underwear, and his body contorted.

He was going full dragon.

I'd never seen anything like it before.

Roxy linked to just me as she rushed out the door. *I'm disappointed we're only getting the rear view. I heard they're huge.*

Can we save the penis conversation for later? The last thing we needed was a distraction when all this shit was about to go down. *I'm sure Lillith would love to be privy.*

Egan's body grew larger and larger until it was roughly the size of a small house. His body took on dark olive-green scales, and his wings sprouted from his back. When it was over, he was the same height as a living room with vaulted ceilings. He took off into the sky, almost black in the darkness.

I breathed deep to catch any odd scents. We'd learned that the fae could hide their flowery smell easily, but they were also arrogant. If they thought there were enough of them, they might be more reckless.

However, nothing seemed out of sorts.

Since the dragon hadn't alerted us to danger, I gestured to the woods, and everyone nodded.

In seconds, we were across the backyard and into the trees. In the darkness, if we hunkered low and stayed near the trees, maybe we'd be harder to find.

The vampires could run as fast as us in human form, so we all flew through the woods. Cassius took the lead with Donovan and me right behind him.

The older vampire knew the woods, helping us move faster without making noise. I wasn't sure how long we'd been running, but the moon was high in the dark sky. It had to be midnight.

A loud growl came from the sky, and Egan swooped down low to our left. Flames blew out of his mouth at a threat.

It had to be the fae.

As he'd instructed before shifting, our group headed right, staying clear of the threat.

A shriek pierced before Egan flapped skyward again. Colorful sparks trailed behind him, almost hitting his backside.

We had to run faster.

Three roars rang in the air like he'd told us he'd do if he created a distraction. I had thought it wouldn't come to this. I'd been so stupid.

"Hurry," Cassius whispered over his shoulder.

No, he shouldn't have spoken. Any nearby supernatural could've heard him.

We were over halfway to Titan's pack. I thought we might make it the entire way, but all hope came crashing down when a fae stepped in front of Cassius.

The vampire grunted and stopped in his tracks, trying not to run into him.

I raised my hand so the others behind us knew to stop. *There's a fae up ahead.*

Shit, what do we do? Axel asked as he and Roxy caught up to us.

"Daddy?" Lillith said with uncertainty as she watched her father stare down the fae.

"Get out of the way, or I'll end you." The fae had dark purple hair that flowed over her shoulders. She was four inches shorter than me, but her eyes held a fierceness I'd never seen before. She was colder than the vampire that had tried to kill Donovan and Axel; never had I faced someone with darker demons.

"What do you want?" Cassius demanded, his voice wavered. "We're just out for a run."

"Shifters aren't the only ones who can detect lies." Her

dark purple eyes landed on me. They were so dark it was as if they were sunken into her face. She was beautifully terrifying. I'd never understood the phrase until now. "Now move. We want her, the filthy half-breed."

She was honest, which wasn't abnormal for fae. Maybe we could learn something from her. "How am I an abomination?"

"We sense the fae inside you, but you're also a wolf." She wrinkled her nose as she stepped past Cassius as if he were inconsequential. "Which means you must die."

"I didn't do anything to deserve death." If they thought I would lie down and take their threats, they'd soon realize how wrong they were. "I've minded my own business my entire life. I don't want anything to do with your kind."

"The fact you think there is an option is problematic." She rubbed her hands together and methodically stepped in my direction. She smirked like she was enjoying the confrontation. "We don't need people from this horrible realm getting any ideas."

Donovan stood in front of me, blocking me from the fae's line of sight. "What kind of ideas are you so afraid of?"

"That you'll create a hybrid and try to live in our realm." The girl shook her head, her hair bouncing from side to side. "That won't happen. We won't allow it. That's why our bloodlines must stay pure. It's bad enough the dragons were tied to our land. Why do you think they're all here now?"

"You aren't getting her." Donovan stuck out his chest and stared the girl down. "Back off."

"I was hoping you'd say that." She chuckled evilly. "Do you all feel the same way?" She scanned the group for someone who might stand down.

"Yes." Lillith spread her legs apart, facing down the evil bitch. "We're family, and we all stand together."

I'd hoped they would back down, but I didn't think the fae would give them an out anyway. Still, it didn't hurt to try. *Roxy and Axel, go back home.* Maybe I could, at least, protect two people.

You better be kidding me. Roxy linked back, rage evident in each word. *I would never leave you like that.* "We're all sticking with her," she told the fae, emphasizing the thought to me.

The other vampires nodded their heads as well.

"So be it." She lifted her fingers to her mouth and whistled loudly. "Prepare to die."

Twenty fae appeared from the surrounding trees. I hadn't been able to sense them at all. They greatly outnumbered our group of twelve, and they were already more powerful.

She lifted her hand, pointed at me, and said, "This time, you won't get out alive."

A fae on my left lifted his hand, aiming a blast of magic at me. I locked my eyes on the beam and tried to let my natural instincts take over. I ducked at the last second, and the magic slammed into the tree, cutting it in two.

The tree toppled over, away from our group.

Loud, rapid footsteps came from the location of Titan's pack. Thank God, they were almost here. It sounded like all their fighters were heading our way. My only concern was whether we could last until they got to us.

The fae attacked everyone in our party. We dodged the magic. I hoped our stamina could keep us safe.

The dark purple warrior fae headed straight at me. "This has gone on long enough." She lifted her hands, palms facing me. Dark purple magic shot for my chest.

I threw my hand up, blocking my body from the blast. I pictured the blast slowing down like the bullet the vampire had shot at me. I wasn't sure what I'd done then, but I was desperate. I concentrated ahead of me, into the purple line. When it didn't work, I closed my eyes, waiting for the blast, but nothing hit me.

"How is that possible?" the purple fae gasped. "That can't be ..."

I slowly opened my eyes and saw the magic dissolve and disappear.

She said louder, "You can't be stronger than me! You're a mutt." She lifted her hands, and magic blasted from her palms.

There was no way I could stop that. It was coming way too fast. I dropped and rolled out of the way. I took a second to survey our group. The fae were taking it easier on them, almost like they were distracting them so the purple fae could end me.

If it kept them safe, I was all for it.

The other shifters arrived and ran into the small area where we fought. Torak ran straight to Donovan and the other shifters, giving them iron as five other shifters made their way to the vampires. Unlike what we'd hoped, we didn't have any shields. There hadn't been enough time. So, they all swung long, round pipes like baseball bats.

The iron was absorbing the magic, so it was working. I'd been afraid it wouldn't work on full-blooded fae.

"This is ridiculous." The dark-purple-haired lady charged me, not bothering to keep her distance any longer. "If you want something done right—"

I pivoted to turn past her, but her hand clamped down on my arm.

Her eyes widened with delight. "There's no getting away."

Her power poured into me, filling me with so much static electricity it was damn overwhelming. I tried jerking away, but I'd already grown weak, and she was too strong.

This was it. This was how I died.

CHAPTER EIGHTEEN

"No!" Winter yelled as something slammed into the purple fae, breaking her grasp on my arm.

I opened my eyes to find Winter on top of the fae, using the iron bar to choke her.

"Mom," I gasped as I stood on my shaky legs.

"What?" Her voice shook as her attention went from the fae to me. "What did you just call me?"

That was all the fae needed to shove Winter off. She fell hard on the ground, losing her grip on the iron.

The fae lifted her hands and sneered at my mother. She said through clenched teeth, "You're the one who created this vile creature. Who is her father?" Purple magic trickled from her palm, proving that the iron had removed a lot of her strength.

"Like I'd ever tell you," Mom spat and rolled onto her knees, going for the iron.

"Not happening." The fae kicked her in the stomach. Her arms gave out, and her body hit the ground again.

This was my chance. I rushed forward and jumped on

the fae bitch's back. I wrapped my arms around her neck and tightened.

She gagged before placing her hands back on my arm. Faint static electricity churned under my skin. The fae was still drained. It didn't feel great, but it was tolerable. I only wished I knew how to return the favor, but that part of me remained a huge mystery.

The fae ducked forward, and I flew over her head. I landed hard on my back with a loud thud. They were stronger and sturdier than I'd given them credit for.

Mom stood and ran over, picking up the iron bar.

"Oh no you don't," the fae rasped and ran toward her.

Before she could get too far, I grabbed her foot and yanked her backward. Her body hit the ground next to me.

Wings flapping overhead caught my attention, and Egan headed toward us, ready to land. Flames flickered from his mouth, and his golden eyes took in the chaos.

"We need to retreat," the fae yelled as she stood.

I looked over my shoulder to find we had the clear advantage. Donovan swung a metal pole at a fae and ran straight toward me.

The few fae who were still fighting had lost most of their power.

"Now!" the purple-haired one screamed again. "Before we can't transport."

Right as Mom swung the pole at the purple fae, she disappeared. Mom wound up striking air.

Donovan wrapped his arms around me and asked, "Are you okay?"

I looked over his shoulder. The other fae vanished one by one right before Egan touched down. Finally, my world stilled from their influence. The only thing out of sorts was the uncomfortable foreign magic the purple fae had pushed into me. But if that was the worst thing that came from the battle, I'd take it.

"Yeah, I'm fine." I hugged him back. "But this isn't over. They'll be back again." They'd keep coming until I was dead.

Titan held his piece of iron like a sword. "Are we sure they're all gone?"

"Yes." I hated to leave Donovan's embrace, but we needed to get back to the house and figure out our next steps. I refused to wait for the next attack. It was time to be proactive. "I don't feel their presence."

"Are you sure you're fine?" Mom rushed over to me and touched my shoulder. "I saw how much magic she attacked you with."

"What?" Donovan growled. "You got hurt."

I glared at Mom, the traitor. "Yes, but Mom saved me, and I'm already feeling much better."

"God, I never thought I'd hear that." Mom placed a hand on her heart. "It sounds so much better than I thought it would."

Egan grunted and flapped his wings. He jerked his head toward the vampires' mansion.

He wanted to go shift back into his human form. Seeing as he couldn't communicate with us, I didn't blame him. "Sure, we'll be back there in a second."

Axel flipped his iron pole in his hand. "I have to say, this was freaking awesome. All my baseball days paid off."

"You mean the one game you played?" Donovan lifted a brow at him. "And you stomped off the field when they tagged you out at first base."

They had stories about each other like Roxy and I did.

"Aw, don't feel bad, honey." Roxy patted his arm. "You're a home run for me."

"Do you think she hears how cheesy she sounds right now?" Lillith asked Katherine.

Katherine grinned. "Leave them alone. They're cute."

Torak lowered the metal to his side. "What else should we do?"

"I think we're good." Titan glanced at me. "Maybe you should stay at the pack."

Cassius shook his head. "No, our food supply is at the mansion. We need to stay at the house. Maybe some of you can stay with us. We have food now that Sadie and her friends stay there."

Mom jumped at the opportunity. "I can do that."

"That means I will too." Titan gestured at himself and Torak. "And him."

"We have plenty of rooms to accommodate whomever you want or need." Dawn stood by her husband. "It's been nice to have a house full of people again."

"Then it's settled." Titan turned to his pack. "You all head back and get some rest. There's no telling when the fae will come back. We need to rest and get ready to fight. Tell Billy to make those shields now."

"Got it." An older pack member saluted, and Titan's pack headed back to their homes.

Cassius walked toward the mansion, and the rest of us followed his lead.

Even though I knew the fae were gone, I scanned the trees and listened for any odd sounds.

The others did the same, and no one made a noise on the return trip.

The mansion came into view with Egan pacing out back as he waited for us. His shoulders tensed, and deep lines were etched into his forehead.

When we were a few feet from him, Athan asked, "What's wrong?"

Egan looked directly at me. "We can't keep doing the same thing."

A low growl left Donovan. "What the hell does that mean?"

"That they're going to keep coming until I'm dead." Everyone had to understand that. "Every time they come, they bring a bigger army. We can't fight them off much longer."

"But we have iron now." Mom raised her hand holding the iron. "We're good."

"Iron won't do us any good if they bring a hundred fae next time." They could easily overwhelm us. "We have to be smart."

"We don't have much of an option here." Donovan took my hand and turned me to face him. "You heard Cassius. There isn't another way."

"And you aren't leaving us." Roxy scowled at me. "If you're thinking of becoming a martyr, it's not happening."

"No, I'm not." I knew that clearly. Neither she, Winter, nor Donovan would allow that. They'd guard my room all night if they had to.

"I wouldn't be so sure," Egan interjected. "She said some crazy things back at Titan's."

If I could kick his ass, I would. "I told you I wasn't planning anything stupid." Asshole.

"The only choice we have is to find a fae," Cassius said, reeling us in. "And they are very hard to find here."

"I know where one is." The girl from the bathroom back at Kortright flashed in my mind. "I met one on campus."

"You did?" Roxy's brows furrowed. "I don't remember meeting one."

"It was the night after I met Donovan for dinner." The girl's teal hair and sad eyes were burnt into my brain. "I ran to the bathroom before going to the dorm room. Lillith and Katherine were hanging out with you."

Lillith gestured at me. "Is that why you looked a little off?"

"Please," Roxy scoffed. "She always looks a little off."

Katherine smacked Roxy and muttered, "Not helping."

"No, I probably looked strange because when I touched the girl, something popped inside me." Now I realized what that must have been. "I think she inadvertently unlocked my fae magic. That's when I started doing those odd things."

"True, I'd never seen you stop a bullet before." Roxy nodded. "Or disappear right in front of my face."

"Fae aren't inclined to help those outside their race." Mom looked at me sternly. "That is a very risky move."

"Rook and you found a ..." I paused, looking for the right word. I didn't want to upset Titan. "... friendship, so there are some fae out there that are open to it."

"But he came here looking to connect with humans and other supernaturals." Winter dropped the rod and walked over to me. "Most aren't like that."

"The girl at Kortright was at a human school too." She had to see there were some similarities. "Maybe they have the same goals."

"Honey, she's made up her mind." Titan stepped next to his mate and looked at her lovingly. "You must see that."

"But that doesn't mean I can't try to change her mind." Mom removed her arm from his grip. "She could be walking into a trap or worse."

"It can't get worse than what's going on here." I had a feeling they'd bring unlimited resources in their next attack.

"At the university, they can't attack us out in the open like here. There would be humans all around."

"She's right," Egan said slowly. "That might be our only chance to save ourselves."

"I don't like it." Donovan huffed and looked at me, nibbling on his bottom lip. "But if that's what Sadie thinks we should try, I'm for it."

"The only problem is, we can't all go with her." Luther's tone held an edge of hysteria. "I mean ... the humans."

"No, we wouldn't want everyone to go." The fewer people we brought, the fewer people we had to worry about. "I'm thinking maybe a handful."

"We came here together." Lillith gestured to the seven of us who'd met at Kortright. "We go back together. I'd like to get a few pieces of clothing back anyway."

It always came back to clothes with her, which was odd. She only wore black. You wouldn't think she'd get so attached to her clothes.

"I'll tag along as well." Mom lifted her chin. "I can't sit back and have something else happen to my daughter without me there beside her."

"We don't have any room in the van," Roxy whined. "I had to ride on the floorboard the entire way here, because some large ass," she said and looked at Donovan accusingly, "was taking up the whole backseat."

Donovan rolled his eyes. "Excuse me for being on the brink of death."

"It's about time you apologized." Roxy fluffed her hair. "I was wondering if you ever would."

"Honey, he didn't—" Axel started.

Mom cut him off. "You do realize I have my own car."

"Where she goes, I go." Titan crossed his arms. "Torak, you'll need to stay back and man the pack."

"Man ..." Torak pouted. "I was hoping to see what college is all about."

Mom glanced at me. "When are we heading out?"

"First thing in the morning." I wanted to go now, but it was pointless. We'd get there right around eight in the morning, which would make finding the teal-haired fae harder. We'd have better luck around dusk. "We can all get a good night's rest and head out after lunch."

"I guess we better get some sleep, then." Donovan took my hand and led me to the house. The others followed behind, and ten minutes later, I was curled up in Donovan's arms and falling fast asleep.

AT SIX IN THE EVENING, Lillith pulled the van into the campus parking lot. Mom and Titan followed behind in an older Honda Accord, and we parked far away from the building in the last two spots.

The seven of us climbed out of the van and joined Mom and Titan at the back of their car.

Roxy rubbed her hands together. "What's the plan?"

"Find the fae." It was really that simple. "There shouldn't be too many people wandering around with teal hair and matching eyes."

"Do you think your dad could still be around here?" Lillith asked as she pocketed her keys. "I'd hate to run into him again. We didn't part on the best of terms."

"Wait ..." Axel said with a strained tone. "Your dad could be here?"

I didn't blame him. "First off, it's Tyler." It had been easy to stop calling him Dad. "And secondly, I doubt it. I'm sure they didn't expect us to come back, and I bet Brock left alongside him." Brock had only come here because of me—well, technically Tyler. He'd wanted me as his mate to align himself with Tyler's pack. It had been a power play, which meant the two of them were perfect for each other.

"If she's fae, she should be drawn to the woods." Egan scanned around us. "Let me go shift, and I'll scout the woods."

"Okay." His flying came in handy. "How about the rest of us split up and scope out the campus? She has to be here somewhere."

The main campus was made up of eight buildings. We'd driven past the stadium on the way in, and there had been no one around. We'd stopped and walked around it, but the scents had been old. The other seven buildings consisted of the women's and men's dorms, which abutted the parking lot, the library, and the lecture halls. The women's dorm sat between the combination library and gym, and directly in front of the women's dorm was the Student Center.

The remaining three buildings formed an oval sidewalk connected to the Student Center. Grey Hall was the English building across the terrain from the Student Center. Then Webster Hall, the science building, was to the left, between the Student Center and Grey Hall. Webster Hall was also adjacent to the woods, and Wilson Hall was directly across from Webster.

"Katherine and I will take the women's dorm." That was where I'd seen the fae, and my gut told me we should go there. I wanted to be the one to find her. "We'll check each floor."

"Hey." Donovan frowned. "I thought we'd go together."

"Having a guy patrolling the women's dorm wouldn't be very smart." I needed him to see logic. "Katherine and I are the best bet."

"What do I need to do?" Roxy pointed at herself.

"However we split up, one pack member should be with each group." We had to be strategic. "That way, if one of us finds her, we can alert the others."

"Dammit, you're right," Donovan agreed, even though he wasn't happy. "Winter, why don't you come with me? We can scope out the Student Center, and you can go into the women's bathroom."

Winter kissed Titan on the cheek. "That works."

"Then, I guess, Titan, you're with me." Axel didn't sound thrilled. "We'll take the tree line and check the library and Webster Hall."

"That means Lillith and I will check out Grey and Wilson Hall," Roxy said and grabbed the vampire's arm. "Let's get this over with. I'm ready to get back to the mansion."

Our group split up, and Katherine and I headed straight to the dorm.

"Do you have a plan?" she asked as we entered the main doors.

"Nope. I'm hoping my magic will tell me something." Maybe I'd get dizzy if we got near her. "Let's take the stairwell."

We scanned one floor after another. All of them buzzed with the stress of exams, gossip of who's screwing who, and any other shenanigans they found important. It reinforced that I would never be close to human. How I wished stuff like that was important instead of my impending death if we didn't find the fae.

I'd thought we'd stumble upon the fae in minutes, but we'd been looking for over thirty minutes without a hint of anything.

Katherine opened the door to the top floor and waved me through. "This is the last stop."

We walked down the hallway just like all the others. Most of the doors were open, and the scent of flowers was lacking.

Any luck? I linked to the others. Hopefully, someone had picked up a trail.

Nothing. Donovan connected. *I wish I had something different to report, but the Student Center is clean.*

Same here with us, Roxy complained. *We've barely seen other students.*

We've only smelled a wolf, Axel replied. *And Egan informed us he's checking the men's dorm just in case, but he didn't find anything in the woods.*

Wolf? My heart rate increased. *Is it Tyler?*

I don't know. Axel sounded paranoid. *I've never smelled this one before.*

Great. This was just great. *Has Titan? What does he have to say?*

No, it's not him. Relief was evident in Axel's voice. *Thank God.*

A flowery scent hit me, and my heart raced. *I think I smell her.* "Katherine, down here." I hurried down the hall and came to the last door on the left. The sweet scent was strong. It had to be her.

I knocked on the door loudly. When it didn't open after a few seconds, I pounded on it harder. Right before I finished, it opened, and I nearly tumbled into the room.

The fae's teal eyes widened, and her face was set into a hard frown. "What the hell are you doing here?"

CHAPTER NINETEEN

The fae didn't strike me dead immediately, giving me a small glimmer of hope. "Look, I'm not here to cause trouble."

"Really?" Her eyes flicked to the hallway. "It sure doesn't look like it."

All my hope vanished. The only reason I was still standing was because of the humans all around. "Can we come in for a second?" I gestured to Katherine. "So we can talk?"

"My roommate is here." The sulfuric tell of a lie filled my nose. "Now's not a good time."

"You're lying." She should have known better. I hated to force her into something, but my hands were tied. "If you don't invite me, I'll let myself in."

"Typical shifter alpha shit." She blew her longish teal bangs out of her eyes, the gesture somehow emphasized the gold-pink hue of her skin. "Fine. Come in." She opened the door wider and waved us in.

I rushed into the room, worried about the new shifter Axel and Titan had smelled. There was no telling who it was. The possibilities were endless—someone from Tyler's pack, Brock, or even a student we'd never crossed paths with before. However, I'd come this far, and the damage was done. I wouldn't leave without at least attempting to hide from the fae. After all, that was the whole point of coming here.

She shut the door and glared. "Do you realize how much trouble I could get in by you being here?" Her sweet, vulnerable façade I'd seen in our prior meeting was gone.

"Look, I'm sorry. I'm not trying to get you into trouble." I hadn't even considered that possibility, but it made sense. "I'm just desperate and was hoping you'd be willing to help."

"What exactly do you want me to do?" She tilted her head like I was a puzzle. "I'm already risking a lot by not making you leave."

"Did you alert the fae to Sadie?" Katherine asked, her dark brown eyes shooting daggers. "She said something happened when she touched you."

Katherine stepping in shocked me. She usually went with the flow, but for her to interject like that meant more to me than she'd ever know.

"What? No." The fae shook her head. "I would never. But when she touched me ..." She trailed off.

The human who had interrupted our conversation in the bathroom that night had said her name. I wracked my brain, trying to remember it. If I used it, maybe I would come off as more friendly. "Naida ..." I prayed that was her name.

When she looked at me, I knew it had to be right, so I continued, "They're after me. That's why we're here. What put me on their radar?"

She closed her eyes and shook her head. "When you touched me, you set your fae side free."

"Why would you let her do that?" Katherine's forehead lined with confusion. "Was that the point?"

"How many times do I have to tell you no?" Naida said a little too loudly for the dorms. She sucked in air. "I was upset, and I didn't really know she was fae until she'd already touched me."

I was missing something. "Why didn't they attack me here?"

"Because my magic hid yours." Naida walked past her desk and sat on her bed. "They only sensed you after you'd left campus. Why did you do that?"

"It was for survival. The man I thought was my father tried to kill my fated mate." It didn't matter, though. "He was going to make me leave here regardless."

"Dammit." She ran a hand through her hair. "If you stay here, you should be okay."

"Tyler, the man who raised me, is looking for me." I had a feeling whoever Axel had smelled was associated with him. "I can't stay. That's why I'm here. I need your help."

"You want me to hide your fae magic?" She laughed hard. "I'm surprised you know it's possible."

"I have very old and strong friends." She didn't need to know more than that. "They figured it out."

"If I do that, it'll use the last of my reserves." She tapped her foot on the ground. "And that means I'll have to go back home to recharge."

I figured she'd be dying to go back home. "I thought fae didn't like being in this realm."

"I do prefer home, but my goal was to come here and learn." She licked her lips. "It's part of my future."

"Then you can visit with your family for a few days." Katherine shrugged. "I don't see the problem."

"Fine." She stood and flexed her fingers like she was preparing for a fight. "I just didn't want my family to bombard me with questions about what's going on here, but it's inevitable."

I tensed. I'd wanted this, but her willingness worried me. What if this was a trick? At least, this way, everyone I loved or cared about wouldn't get hurt. It would be a complete takedown or just me.

"Do you want me to do this or not?" Naida dropped her hand. "You need to decide and fast. My magic is about gone."

"Yes, I want you to." I had to push my fear aside; it was the only option. "Just last time someone did that to me, it didn't feel great."

She walked toward me slowly. "Who did this to you?"

"Some dark-purple-haired fae girl." Just thinking about it made my skin crawl. "They attacked us last night."

"Must have been Ensley." Naida chewed on a nail. "She's part of the fae army. They really are going after you."

"Did you think I was lying?" My anger bled through. I couldn't believe she thought I'd manipulate her like that. "They aren't fond of half breeds."

"No, they aren't." Naida pursed her lips. "But it's interesting that they're going so hard so fast. I bet it has to do with Tyler."

All things led back to him. "I ran away because of him. It's not like I want to follow in his footsteps or anything."

"My kind really doesn't care." She waved a finger around. "We don't see gray, only black and white. Sometimes, this realm makes things so complicated. They see you as having ties to Tyler, and you have fae magic. You're a threat."

"Why are you willing to help me, then?" The more she said, the more nervous I got.

"Because you were kind to me." She pointed at Katherine. "Even this vampire doesn't trust me and is itching to leave."

"Who says I'm not wanting to leave?" I wasn't feeling too warm and fuzzy with her right now.

"Oh, you aren't." Naida grinned. "You're uncomfortable, but you aren't discriminating against me. That says a lot."

"Then why don't you get to helping her?" Katherine said with annoyance. "We need to leave before Tyler finds us."

"You're right." She lifted her hand again, and teal magic bubbled in her palm. "I don't need anyone stopping by and finding you here with me either." She reached for me but paused. "This won't feel comfortable, but you need to stay still. I don't have any magic to spare. Also, if you use your magic again, you'll reveal yourself."

I sucked in a breath and nodded. "Okay." I didn't even know how to use the magic, so it would be a blessing not to have to try.

She touched my arm, and her magic poured inside me. The static electricity coursed under my skin, but it wasn't nearly as painful as the purple fae's magic. Her magic didn't feel foreign, though. It almost felt the same as mine, only slightly different.

Her magic soaked into my skin where my own fae magic flowed. It connected with mine and twirled. The two strands danced together, weaving in and out of each other.

"Are you okay?" Katherine whispered.

Whatever was going on had left me unable to respond. The connection between the two of us was too much. I barely nodded my head, hoping she saw the motion. I didn't need her getting scared and overreacting.

Naida's magic followed mine. I felt it under my skin. It ran inside my body, leaving a residue on top of mine. She was coating my magic.

I wasn't sure how long we stood like that, but once her magic had run through me entirely, the intensity receded. As her magic pulled back, I opened my eyes.

"Who are you?" Naida asked, her voice shaking. "Is this a joke?"

"No." I didn't need to lose her kindness now. "I don't know what you're talking about."

"Your magic...." She dropped her hand and blinked. "Who's your father?"

"How do you know my father is the fae?" That didn't sit well with me.

Her eyes darkened. "Just tell me his name."

"Rook." There was no point in pretending.

Donovan linked with me. *We need to go. A few wolves are gathering outside the Student Center. We're getting the car. You need to run out of the back of the women's dorm in a few minutes.*

Have they found any of us? My heart raced. I needed more time with Naida. She knew something about me.

Not yet, but they caught Winter's and my scents. Donovan sounded concerned. *I'm coming to you now.*

No, that would be bad. I needed to remain calm so the others didn't freak out more. *You might bring them here. The best thing is to lead the scent to the car. We should be out of here before they can pick up anyone else's trail.*

She's right, Roxy agreed, trying to calm Donovan's natural mate tendencies. *It could be worse if you go to her.*

Fine, he growled with displeasure. *But if you aren't out there when we pull up to the women's dorm, my ass is coming for you.*

That's fair. His fierce loyalty rang true. It was so different from Tyler and Brock and so damn welcoming. *I'll be there.*

"Rook is your dad?" Her eyes widened, and she blew out a breath. "That can't be."

Loud running footsteps broke through my concentration. A few girls squealed as whoever it was came barreling down the hallway.

"Shit, we have to go." I had a feeling they were looking for me. "The wolves are coming."

"Great." Katherine glanced around. "What the hell do we do?"

"I can transport you to the stairwell a floor below, but that's all I have left." Naida stared at the door. "Then I'll have to go back to Fae before I can't even do that."

That should buy us a little time. "That would be enough." Right now, Katherine and I were screwed. We couldn't make it out of here without her help. "Let's go."

She touched both Katherine and me, and within seconds, we appeared in the stairwell a floor down.

"Oh, God." Katherine moaned and dropped to the floor. "I'm going to puke."

"I wish I could do more." Naida pulled me into a hug. "Stay safe. I'll find you soon." And she disappeared.

Why the hell had she hugged me? And what was with the warm attitude after she'd freaked out on me? I shook my head and focused on the task at hand.

"Katherine." I bent down and felt her cool forehead. "I

get you don't feel well, but we have to get moving. We want to have a huge lead on them."

"Yeah." She stood on wobbly legs. "Now I get how you feel when the fae appear."

"It's awful, but here, put your arm around me, and I'll support some of your weight." I didn't want to freak her out, but we had to get our asses going. *Guys, there are wolves here.*

Katherine followed my instructions, and we took the first step down to the exit.

What do you mean by here? Donovan sounded downright scary. *Are they near you?*

Yes. They picked up my scent and almost found me in Naida's room. Every time I tried to speed up, Katherine would stumble and almost make us fall. We wouldn't make it out of here if she didn't pick up her pace. *Naida transported us down a set of stairs, but Katherine isn't doing well. We're slowly making our way to the first floor.*

I'm on my way. Donovan locked down our bond.

Dammit. I didn't want him to get caught too. *Roxy, stop him.*

Girl, you know I can't do that. She sounded aggravated. *Maybe coming here was a big mistake.*

Naida hid me, so at least, our original goal got taken care of. If we made it out of here intact, I'd consider it a win. As long as we could get back to the mansion, we could regroup without the constant threat of a fae attack. *I have no clue how many shifters are here.*

The door to the top floor banged open, and running footsteps hit the stairwell.

No. I glanced at the stairwell. We were only on floor nine. This wouldn't work. I opened the door to the rooms and trudged Katherine through it.

Thankfully, she picked up her pace.

"Let's go to the elevator. It might be our best chance." I ran fast, dragging Katherine behind me. She stumbled over her feet, but I didn't give a damn. Time was of the essence.

Some girls yelled as we ran by, startling them.

Great, this would alert the shifters to our location. I reached the elevator and pushed the down button.

The elevator was on the floor already, and the doors immediately opened.

"Come on." I grabbed Katherine and pulled her in after me. I pressed the "close" button and hit the first floor. "I don't care how sick you feel; when we get there, run fast and hard."

"Got it." Katherine leaned against the wall and took deep breaths. "I'm starting to feel better."

"Good. Don't focus on feeling bad." Every second we stayed here meant we came even closer to being captured. The elevator bell pinged, alerting us that we were on the second floor. "Get ready."

The elevator stopped, and the doors slowly opened to reveal Brock and some random guy standing there, waiting for me.

CHAPTER TWENTY

Brock smirked at me. "Look what we just found."

"The pink hair gave her away as soon as the van pulled in," the guy beside him said. His shaggy, mousy hair fell into his bland brown eyes. For a shifter, he wasn't very strong or attractive, which made it easier for him to blend into the background. His wolf didn't have the strength of an alpha or beta; I could feel it from here.

I linked with the pack. *Brock is here.*

Where is here? Donovan asked. *He's with you?*

Yes. I needed to keep calm and pretend to be weak. I had to catch them off guard. *He was waiting for us outside the elevator.*

Shit, Donovan growled. *I'm coming.*

No, don't. The last time something like this went down, Tyler and Brock had almost killed Donovan. I couldn't risk it again. *Is the parking lot empty? Do you see any cars that stick out?*

There are some expensive-looking black ones. He paused for a second. *With Tennessee license plates for Hamilton County.*

They're Brock's pack. His pack lived on Lookout Mountain. *We need to hit the woods.*

There's no way in hell I'm leaving you, Donovan growled. *I mean it.*

Then get Mom and Titan to bring our cars around. Besides, if Tyler finds out Mom is here, there's no telling what he'll do. Titan wouldn't let Mom leave without him, especially with all of these other shifters around. Besides, we had two vehicles. *If they can slip away, we can meet them where Lillith did last time.*

The elevator door slid closed, but Brock grabbed my arm and pulled me away from the elevator.

I turned my focus back to Brock. I already knew the answer, but I needed to hear it from his lips. "What are you doing here?" I scanned the room and realized it was oddly quiet. Only one human sat in the corner with earbuds in her ears as she worked on her computer.

He chuckled. "Isn't it obvious?"

"Stop it." I tried weakly to pull my arm from his grasp. "I'm not something you can just yank around."

"Oh, but you are." He got into my face. "You were promised to me, and nothing will change that."

This had been my worry about coming back here, but my death would have been imminent if we hadn't. I'd thought that Brock and Tyler would've given up on me returning to the university. Apparently, they hadn't.

"Let her go," Katherine hissed lowly. "Now."

"That's not how this works." Brock snapped his fingers. "Tommy, handle her."

"Yes, sir." Tommy grabbed Katherine by the neck and growled, "Don't make a move or I'll break it."

Katherine's eyes widened in surprise. I couldn't blame her, though.

I hadn't expected someone like Tommy to do that either. He didn't seem like he had the guts, but we were wrong. Desperation and power could make even the weakest try to look strong. "You realize there is a human here."

"Who is really preoccupied." Brock's breath hit me right in the face. "I'm not too concerned."

It smelled like ass, and I wanted to gag. "We aren't alone."

"Do you think I don't know that?" He laughed hard as two shifters stepped from the stairwell. "I have adequate backup, so don't worry."

Egan strengthened our group tenfold. "Okay." I didn't want to argue. For him to be so cocky, there was no telling how many others he had patrolling the area.

Donovan linked to our pack. *Winter said okay, but she isn't happy about being the chauffeur. Axel, send Titan this way. I'm going inside the dorm to get Sadie and Katherine out.*

No, I have a plan. I refused to dangle Donovan in front of Brock. That would make Brock more irrational and dangerous. *Everyone, meet me in the woods. I'll get Katherine and me out.*

Displeasure waved off him. *If you aren't there in five minutes, my ass is coming to get you.*

And my happy ass will be right there with him, Roxy chimed in.

I'll be there. But first, I needed more information.

My attention went back to Brock. "How did we not smell you?" I'd thought we'd have seen this coming.

"Because Tommy hung around the school." Brock tightened his hold on my arm. "No one you knew could be here or you'd have been tipped off immediately. Tommy's been gunning for a higher spot in my pack. It was a win for both of us. He's proved himself useful."

"I knew I wouldn't let you down." Tommy smiled and tightened his grip on Katherine's neck.

She gagged.

"Please stop." I hated to beg, but I had to totally disarm him before I struck. "She has nothing to do with this. It's between you and me."

Where the hell are you? Axel said in a panic. *I'm coming to get you.*

Don't you dare come here, Roxy chastised. *We're heading that way. They didn't catch us, and we're going around, so come behind Webster Hall.*

Their argument sounded much like mine and Donovan's. *Hurry, Roxy. I'm about to kick Brock's ass, but I need to wait until you're close enough for everyone to meet up and run.*

I turned to Brock, not wanting him to get suspicious. "Just let her go."

"You've got to be joking," he spat. "She helped you run away. Her mere existence insults me."

"You tried to get her to drink blood straight from a dying human." He wasn't the victim here. "What did you expect? She wasn't going to be thrilled to work with you."

"I was trying to make her strong," Brock sneered. "But she obviously didn't appreciate it."

"You tried to get her to lose her humanity." Tyler and Brock had never had any humanity, or if they had, it disappeared a long time ago. "Not many people want to give that up." Giving up our humanity made vampires turn into monsters with only greed and power ruling them. There was no happiness. That loss caused them to keep searching for something more to fulfill them because nothing did.

"Humanity holds people back," he barked and turned to the two wolf shifters. "Anything out of sorts?"

"Two have picked up another wolf smell," one of the guys answered as the two headed our way.

We were running out of time.

Roxy linked with me. *Okay, I'm here. We're all in front of the library, and Egan is overhead.*

One of your scents got caught. We had to hurry before they tracked them down. This could all be over if Katherine and I didn't get out of here. *We'll be there in a second.*

"You should thank me for killing that worthless human you were fawning over." Brock wrinkled his nose. "He could never give you what I could." He ran a finger along my jaw.

I closed my eyes, trying to keep the contents of my stomach down. I had to be smart. "You're right." Donovan could give me love and support, things Brock could never provide. I leaned forward as if to kiss him.

"Thank God, you've finally come to your senses," he said and lowered his lips to mine, startling me.

Slobber poured down my chin, and his tongue forced its way into my mouth and flailed around like crazy. This time, I couldn't hold back the gag.

I pushed him off me, and his brows furrowed in confusion. I punched him hard in the face. The sound of bone cracking filled the air, and he fell to his knees, grabbing his jaw.

"Brock!" Tommy yelled as his attention turned away from Katherine and focused on his alpha heir.

The other two shifters rushed toward us, eliminating the last ten feet rapidly.

Katherine kneed her captor in the crotch. He fell to the ground next to Brock, cradling his balls.

I turned on my heel, took her hand, and dragged her toward the door. The other two were breathing down our necks. "Go open the door."

She sprinted to the door as I turned to face the two assholes. I had to think of something to get out of this situation. I glanced around. Four girls were heading toward the door. Katherine opened it and waved them in.

Yes! Brock and Tommy couldn't do much with them here and watching. "Leave me alone." I channeled all my anger and frustration into my words. I wiped the remaining slobber off my face, letting it fuel me even more. "He cheated on me, and now you two are trying to bully me into being with him."

The four girls stopped in their tracks to watch the drama unfold. That was the thing about humans: they loved the dramatics, and their television shows proved it.

"Now listen here," the taller one growled. "You're coming with us." He tried to say it low, but I wouldn't let it go. Did he think I was an idiot?

"No, I won't go with you." I stepped back like I was scared. "Don't make me."

"Sadddiiieee," Brock slurred, both hands clutching his jaw. "Git ak her."

"You four, leave her alone." One of the human girls pulled her phone from her pocket. "Or I'm calling security."

Brock glowered at me. I'd never seen him look at anyone with so much hate before. It both scared and empowered me.

"Thank you." I turned my back on the four guys, emphasizing that I'd won temporarily. They wouldn't let me get far.

I rushed out the door with Katherine on my heels. We took off toward the tree line, ready to get to safety.

We ran past the library, and five feet from the woods, I heard footsteps pounding in our direction. There were so many I couldn't count them all.

I stepped into the trees and ran into something tall and hard. Large arms wrapped around me, and the smell of musky rain hit my nose.

Lillith blurred as she appeared next to me and wrapped her arms around her best friend. "Katherine, I was so scared. Are you okay?"

"Yeah." She sounded hoarse, but not nearly as bad as I'd been afraid.

You scared the shit out of me. Donovan bent his head down and stopped. *Why do I smell another man on you?*

Brock kissed me, but we don't have time for that. I looked at the others, panic coursing through me. "We've got to go."

I'm going to kill that jackass. Donovan stepped around me, heading back toward campus. *Slowly.*

Stop. He had to get his head on straight. "We've got to go. Now."

"Come on, man." Axel pulled on Donovan's shoulder. "They've got an army heading this way."

Donovan sucked in a breath and turned. "Fine, but this isn't over."

Right as we turned to head toward the vehicles, ten shifters came into view.

"Run!" I yelled.

Our group charged forward, but it was too late. More wolf shifters ran in our direction, and the ten pushed themselves harder to catch up to us.

The trees flew past as we raced to Mom and Titan, but in my heart, I knew they would be on us in seconds.

Wings flapped overhead, alerting me to Egan's presence. I risked a glance skyward and found him in his complete dragon form. I wasn't sure if that comforted me or not. For him to go full dragon, we must have been under a threat similar to the fae.

The vampires ran in front, and Donovan and I took up the rear. The narrow pathway only allowed for two of us to pass at a time. The vampires were the fastest, so they weren't our holdup. Our human forms slowed us, but if we stopped and shifted, they'd catch up.

We won't make it. We were only about a mile from campus, and the enemy wolves were nipping at our heels. *We have to fight.*

Keep going, Donovan said, trying to encourage me. *They have more people than us.*

I heard someone lunge, and arms wrapped around my waist. I fell onto my knees.

Sadie! Roxy cried as she turned around to help me. *Get up.*

But there was no use. Donovan ran toward me and punched the guy in the ear. The guy groaned and released his hold. Another shifter attacked Donovan.

We were screwed, and we had no way to tell Mom or Titan.

I heard bones crack as Axel and Roxy shifted into their wolf forms, and Lillith's and Katherine's sweet smell grew stronger as they turned back to help us.

This had been a fucking suicide mission. I'd tried to protect the people I loved and cared about, and all I'd done was put them in a situation that was just as bad if not worse. If they got hurt because of me, I could never forgive myself.

Axel lunged and bit into the neck of the shifter attacking Donovan. Ten more wolf shifters ran into the mix, all of them in wolf form. Each girl had three attackers, and Donovan and Axel had four each.

My three attackers were in human form. Their goal wasn't to kill me, just render me useless. I turned to find Donovan shifting into his wolf, his black fur sprouting across his arms.

"Come with us now," the tall shifter from back at the dorm growled. He clutched my arm and dragged me back toward the dorm.

No, I couldn't separate from the group. I swung at him, but he caught my hand before it could connect with his face.

"Tsk." He chuckled. "I saw what you did to Brock back there. You won't get the slip on me."

Another guy bent down, grabbed my waist, and threw me over his shoulder, my face smashing into a backpack. He stepped toward school, and I did the only thing I could think to do. I lowered my head, aimed for his side where the backpack ended, and sank my teeth into his waist.

"Ow!" he yelled and tried throwing me to the ground, but I held on tight, letting my teeth thrash his skin before hitting the ground hard.

"I know he said to bring her unharmed." A short, stocky guy glowered at me. "But I refuse to let a little bitch take me down." He grabbed me by the hair and yanked, cracking my neck.

A low, threatening growl came from behind us. I watched as Donovan tried to reach me, but the four wolves surrounding him took him down ... hard.

"No!" I yelled.

CHAPTER TWENTY-ONE

I spun around and kicked the guy holding me in the nuts. I didn't give a damn about the consequences. I had to get to my mate.

My captor's grasp slackened, and I surged forward before another douchebag could grab me. I couldn't see my mate with all four wolves covering him.

Right as I reached Donovan, Egan landed a few feet away from me. Thank God. We needed backup and bad.

My claws extended, and I dug them into the wolf right on top of Donovan. The enemy wolf's mouth was dangerously close to my mate's neck. As my nails dug into his skin, the dark brown wolf released his hold on my mate and whimpered.

Good. The asshole should feel pain.

I dragged the heavy wolf off Donovan right as someone slammed into me from behind. Hands grabbed my arms, yanking my hands behind my back. Using the moment, I let my claws that were still stuck in the wolf's skin slice as I jerked back.

Egan charged toward the other three enemy wolves, chomped down on one of them, and used his talons to grab the other two. He threw them into trees while the wolf in his mouth shrieked with pain.

The two wolves landed in unnatural positions while the wolf in Egan's mouth became deathly quiet. The fact that only three of them were dead wasn't good enough for me.

Blood poured from deep bite wounds in Donovan's shoulder and leg. The wolves had tried to tear him apart. His chest rose and fell, giving me the peace of mind that he was still alive.

But I needed to hear his voice to make sure. *Donovan?*

Yeah, he groaned. *Are you okay?*

Of course, he'd be worried about me. *Yes, I am. Stay still and heal for a second. Egan is kicking everyone's ass.*

Steeling myself, I slammed the back of my head into the man holding me. The crunch of his nose breaking was music to my ears.

"Ow." He let me go.

I spotted the dark brown wolf who had bitten my mate's shoulder. Raw rage filled me, and I welcomed it. I would kill that asshole. I was sick and tired of people hurting my mate.

I charged toward him, and his eyes widened. He turned and ran back toward the campus.

Nope, not happening. I glanced at my friends, making sure they were all okay. We were still outnumbered, but having Egan on our side was paying off. My friends had formed a tight circle, keeping the threat in front of them.

I didn't need help; it was only one wolf. I'd take him down and come back to help get Donovan to the vehicles.

All of my hesitation vanished as I pursued the fleeing wolf. I tapped into my anger, which allowed me to run faster on two legs than ever before, and I kept up with the animal.

When he glanced over his shoulder at me, he slowed just enough so I could lunge at him. I jumped, aiming for his back.

He rolled to his side, countering my move, and my knees landed on the grassy dirt ground. Pain erupted in my knees, but I ignored it, letting adrenaline take over.

The wolf snarled and went for my arm. I jerked back, but not quick enough. His teeth scratched my skin. Blood trickled down my arm, but the cut was superficial.

I wished I had time to shift, but he'd either attack me while I was vulnerable or run away. It wasn't like I would have time to catch up with him before he got around the other students. A wolf fight in the middle of the courtyard wouldn't be smart.

I stood and spun on my heels, grabbing the fur on the back of the wolf's head. I tugged it back, and he stumbled, but he was too damn sturdy to do much more than that.

He jumped on me, knocking me backward onto the ground, and pressed two paws into my chest.

Heart pounding, I pushed against him, but he kept a firm hold on my chest. I was stuck and couldn't get up. I tried knocking his feet out from under him with my arms, but he was like a freaking statue.

I had to do something. I raised my legs to get them underneath him, but he sat on my knees.

I closed my eyes and waited for him to rip out my throat. My fight was over, and I was at his mercy. But all I felt was his rancid breath hitting me in the face. What was he waiting for?

Footsteps headed our way from the university. No, this

couldn't be happening. I had to get free. I should've never run away from the pack.

Where are you? Donovan linked, his concern wafting through the bond. *I get up and you've vanished.*

I'm trapped. I didn't want to take any of their manpower away, but I was in a bind. *I went after the wolf that bit your shoulder, and he has me pinned. Someone is heading this way.*

Dammit, Sadie, Donovan growled. *I'm on my way.*

No. He was injured. This wouldn't go well. *Is Roxy or Axel available?*

They're busy fighting. Donovan groaned in pain. *Egan is doing most of the work, but there are enough wolves to need everyone.*

Just walking to me was hurting him. He wouldn't get here in time to help me. I bucked again, desperate to get away, and the damn wolf chuckled. I hadn't known that was possible in wolf form. That made me hate the smug ass more.

I lifted my hand toward his neck. It was just out of reach, but I strained to get it. If I could choke him, I could maybe get back to the others before they caught me.

The people were getting closer, and Brock's thick, musky smell hit my nose, confirming my fear. He was coming for me, and this jackass had every intention of holding me here for his alpha heir.

My claws extended again. Maybe this would close the difference. I reached up again, and my nails touched his skin. He tried raising his head higher, lifting some of his weight off my chest.

That was all I needed.

I shifted my weight to one side. He lost his balance and toppled over. I scrambled to my feet and turned back toward my pack. I had to get to Donovan before he got here.

The wolf slammed into my back. I fell forward and landed hard on my knees again. Intense pain spiked through me, and I crashed onto my chest.

"Good job, Pete," Brock said with his usual arrogance. "You got exactly what I needed."

There was no graceful way out of this. I placed my hands on the ground, and right before I could lift myself, Pete sat on my back. I was pinned again, and I couldn't figure out a way to get out of it with Brock here. I could smell three others with him. I was greatly outnumbered. *Donovan, do not come here.* If he showed, Brock would kill him.

Like hell I won't. His voice broke, pain bleeding through. *What's going on?*

Brock's here. I saw no point in lying. He'd find out soon enough. *He'll kill you.*

"Let's get out of here before that dragon finishes the others," Brock said and rubbed his jaw. His injury had healed for the most part, but it still must have been tender. He made it to my side. Next thing I knew, something covered my face, and darkness engulfed me.

The wolf got off me, and rough, strong hands yanked my arms behind my back and slipped cuffs on.

It was blazingly clear—I was their prisoner.

"Get her up!" Brock barked. "We need to get out of here."

The guy grabbed the handcuffs and lifted me. My shoulders moved unnaturally, and I screamed in agony. I linked to the entire pack. *I need your help. Brock has me.*

I can't get there. Donovan sounded broken. *I can barely move.*

I'm on my way, Roxy promised. *We've got her, don't worry.*

Now that I was on my feet, he yanked me forward. I dragged my feet on the ground to slow us all down.

"Pick her up," Brock demanded. "The car is behind the library."

Great, they weren't taking me to a populated area. Even if I cried, the humans wouldn't get there in time. *We're behind the library.*

Roxy replied, *We're almost there.*

My legs came up from under me, and the guy slung me over his back. He took off at a fast run. Each step jarred my body, and my neck popped, shooting pain down my spine. It was obvious he didn't give a crap about the state I was in. His goal was to get me into the car.

I couldn't see a damn thing, and I couldn't bite him because of the bag over my head. For the first time in my life, I felt completely powerless. I prayed to hear the sound of my friends' feet running after me or the sound of Egan flying overhead.

The smell of trees faded, indicating we were out of the woods. We had to be at the library. *Where are you?*

Almost out of the woods, Axel responded. *We should be there in a second.*

Car doors opened in the distance, and we were too close. We'd be at the vehicle in seconds.

I began flailing, trying to do something ... anything to slow the guy down. But it was useless. He wrapped an arm around my back, holding me steady.

Roxy's howl gave me hope.

Roxy linked. *We see you. Do something or we won't reach you in time.*

I can't. They couldn't stop this. The realization sat

heavy on my stomach. *My arms are handcuffed, and I can't make out anything through the bag.*

Cool air conditioning hit my legs as the guy threw me inside the car. Brock's musky smell hit me hard again, and he pulled me close to him. I bucked in the seat, needing to do anything to get out of here.

"Stay still," Brock growled.

The others entered the car as I flopped onto the floorboard.

"Get up." Brock grabbed a fistful of my hair and dragged me back into my seat. "This is pathetic. What would your father say?"

The last guy got in and slammed the door shut, and the tires squealed as they took off. I was too late.

Sadie! Donovan cried. *Roxy. Axel. Go after the car.*

Great, he'd made it here in time to see them drag me away. I wouldn't wish that on anyone. *It's too late unless Egan is nearby.*

No, he was fighting the last few shifters with Lillith and Katherine. Roxy sounded as broken as Donovan. *But I can try.*

Egan couldn't come for me. We were out in public. Humans would see him.

I love you. I had to tell him one last time, in case I never got the chance again. *Always remember.*

I love you too, but this isn't goodbye. I'll find you, Donovan vowed. *And when I do, I'll kill every one of those assholes.*

I shut down the connection, needing to think clearly. It was the only way. "What do you want from me?" I hated being here like this. I couldn't see a thing. It was all black, and even though I could smell five people in the car, I only recognized the scents of Brock, Tommy, and Pete. The other two were a mystery to me.

"This is Tyler's daughter?" A voice I'd never heard before reeked with disgust. "I thought she was supposed to be complaisant."

Great, my reputation preceded me. In all fairness, I'd been that way before Donovan.

"All the great, submissive women had a wild streak at one time." Brock rubbed a hand down my leg. "It's breaking them that's the fun part."

Bile crept up my throat.

"Will I get to help with that?" Another guy chuckled, making my skin crawl.

"What did you just say?" Brock asked lowly.

"Uh ..." The guy stumbled over his words. "I just meant—"

"She's mine." Brock's hand tightened on my thigh. "No one touches what's mine."

If that didn't make me sound like property, I wasn't sure what else would. But I was thankful for his protective stance. I didn't need two sickos after me.

"Got it." The same guy cleared his throat nervously. "I was just kidding."

Yeah, right. The smell of his lie reeked. I was glad I had a barrier.

"Let me be clear. If you touch her," Brock rasped, "I'll kill you."

The car descended into awkward silence.

After a few moments, I inhaled and pretended to cough. "I can't breathe in here. Can you take this thing off me?"

"Oh, no." Brock chuckled. "I won't let your little pack track us down. They'll try anyway, but letting you see where we're taking you would make it that much easier for them."

The determination was clear in his voice. Begging would only rile him up further. The only thing I could do was keep my mouth shut and figure out a way to escape before it was too late.

CHAPTER TWENTY-TWO

The noise of city traffic surrounded the car, adding to my already swimming head from being in this bag for God knew how long. The heavy traffic told me we'd rolled into another large city. It made sense that they'd take me to some sort of city where it would be harder for me to escape. I needed to get out.

I tried moving my arms, but I couldn't feel them. I'd been sitting the entire ride with my hands cuffed behind my back. I'd lost feeling a while ago. Then a realization hit me hard.

I couldn't get out like this. They had me exactly the way they wanted me: stuck.

I opened the link up with the pack. *Is everyone okay?*

It's about damn time, Roxy replied instantly.

We're fine. Donovan's voice broke. *Are you okay?*

Yeah. I needed to be calm for them. Freaking out wasn't going to help anyone. *I'm fine. They haven't hurt me, and we're still on the road.*

Where are you? he asked. *We're following the bond, but it'd be easier if you told us.*

I have no clue. They'd have an idea of what I was going through now. *I still have a bag on my head, and my hands are cuffed. I have no fucking clue where I am or where we're headed.*

Dammit, Donovan growled. *They'll pay for this.*

The car rolled to a stop, and a garage door opened.

Brock touched my shoulder. I jerked away and wound up lying on Tommy, who sat right beside me.

"Stop being difficult," Brock said and dug his fingers into my upper arm. "We're getting out."

The sensation was odd. I could feel his grasp, but not. He wanted to hurt me enough to scare me, but all I felt was pressure. When the circulation returned to my arms, it'd hurt like a bitch.

We're here. I needed to shut down the bond before I fell apart. *I ... I've got to go.*

Sadie ... Donovan warned.

I'll be back soon. I locked it down, not needing a distraction.

After the car pulled into the garage and parked, Brock dragged me across the seat. I tripped to the ground.

"Get up," he said with annoyance. "Do not embarrass me."

"Oh, I'm sorry." I let sarcasm lace each word. He couldn't be serious. "I can't see my surroundings, my arms and hands are numb, and I'm dizzy from the bag that's been over my head."

"Fine," he huffed.

The bag slid off my head, and I blinked a few times, acclimating my eyes to the small, dim, cement garage. "What about my hands?"

"Nope, not happening until we get you situated in your

room," Brock answered, tugging me toward a white door that led into the building, house, whatever it was.

The more I begged, the more he'd get off, so I clamped my lips tight together.

Tommy grinned as he climbed out of the car. "It's nice to be back. I can't wait to see what opportunities you and your dad will offer me since I found the girl."

Probably not what he expected. They would give him a reward that they could easily take away at the earliest convenience. That was how they operated.

Brock opened the door and dragged me behind him. We entered a huge basement with beige walls and off-white carpet. A large couch sat in the center, in front of a flat-screen television with a large pool table behind it. The walls were bare, and the room smelled musty like no one hung out there.

He yanked me toward steep wooden stairs in the far corner of the room.

The farther I entered the house, the more difficult it'd be to escape, but I couldn't run away. Not like this. "Where are you taking me?"

"To your room," he said sharply. "You have a visitor waiting for you."

No, Tyler couldn't be here. Surely not. "Who?"

He increased the pace as we neared the top. "You know who."

We stepped into a den on the main floor. Just like downstairs, there was a large leather couch in the middle of the room that contrasted against the maple floor. The news played on a large flat-screen TV. A dark, cherry wood bar sat in the corner with cabinets full of liquor. I almost jerked to a stop when I found Tyler and Brock's father, Mike, at the table next to it.

Tyler's dark, soulless eyes landed on me, and he ran a hand through his salt-and-pepper goatee, which matched his hair. He was huge, the strongest wolf alpha in the United States, and he ensured his suits always enhanced his muscles. A frown marred his face.

"Ah ... she's here." Mike leaned forward. His hair contained so much gel that it looked plastic, and his beady brown eyes scanned me up and down. His suit was more expensive than Tyler's but didn't fit him as well. Even though he wasn't a small man, the outfit swallowed him. "We were beginning to wonder what was taking so long."

"We hit traffic," Brock grumbled.

"With your future mate cuffed." Brock's father chuckled. "You should be embarrassed."

"You don't—" Brock started.

Tyler cut him off. "If you can't handle her, she shouldn't be your mate."

Did they think I'd changed my mind? I would never mate with Brock. I bit my tongue. Now wasn't the time to declare war.

"He's just joking." Mike laughed loudly. "Uncuff her."

"Yeah, of course." Brock pulled the key from his pocket and jerkily moved to undo the chains. "We wanted to make sure she didn't do something stupid."

"Sure." I couldn't help but goad him. It was all I had. "That's why you did it."

He glared at me with so much hate. However, I preferred that over the times when he looked at me like I was a means to get what he wanted.

With my wrists released, the sensation of sharp needles stabbing my arms overtook me. I winced but channeled the pain inward, not wanting to give these sick sons of bitches the satisfaction.

"Is her room ready?" Brock asked and grabbed my arm, making sure I stayed by him. "If so, I'll take her there."

Tyler answered instead of Mike. "It's ready, but I would like to have the honors if you don't mind. I have a few things I want to talk to my daughter about."

Hearing him call me his daughter made my stomach churn.

Brock released me obediently. "Of course."

Tyler stood and motioned for me to follow. For a second, I considered not obeying, but I needed to show them complacency to have a chance of getting out of here.

I followed him into a hallway and to the first door on the right. I entered an all-white room. The white king-sized bed sat against the far back wall with all-white sheets and a white iced chandelier hanging above it. Even the floor was porcelain. The only color in the entire room was a light gray rug under the bed. There was a large oval mirror in the corner, framed in white, and white curtains along the windows.

Windows.

I rushed over to them. I'd thought I was only one floor up, but it had to be at least three. Maybe the garage was inclined. It wouldn't be easy to get down from here.

The door shut behind me, and I turned to find Tyler's face turning red.

He marched toward me, his jaw clenched. "Do you know how much you've embarrassed me?"

Yes, this was all about him. I wasn't surprised. "It wasn't my intent."

"Fuck intent," he spat in my face. "You're my daughter, and you will obey me."

I didn't respond. I had nothing to add to that.

"You've got nothing to say for yourself?" Tyler ground his teeth.

"Not really." I refused to cower, but I made sure I didn't come off as threatening. "It was something I had to do."

"Something you had to do?" he parroted. He yanked me against his chest. "Well, it's over now. In a week, you will mate with Brock and finally be useful to me."

"I will not." I would refuse. That would never happen. Donovan was it for me.

"Like hell you won't." Tyler smacked me hard on the cheek. My head jerked, and my neck popped. He growled, "I've raised your pathetic ass for eighteen years. This is how you will make it up to me. This is why I kept you, unlike the others."

Fine, if this was how he wanted to do this, I could be cruel too. "I'm not your daughter, so by mating me off to Brock, you'll gain nothing." There, let him be caught off guard for once.

An evil smile spread across his face. "As if I didn't know that." He laughed, and my blood ran cold.

"What?" If he knew that, then why had he kept me?

"When I saw your pink fae hair, I knew." Tyler stepped toward me. A darkness surrounded him. He was colder than I'd thought. He didn't have a heart. "I blamed the witch because a fae-wolf hybrid should produce a male heir worthy to lead ... a force to be reckoned with. An heir who can not only elevate me leading all the supernaturals on Earth but the fae realm as well."

"Did my mother die?" I wanted to see if he smelled differently by telling me the truth.

"Oh, I planned to kill her." Tyler sucked in a breath. "I dreamed of stabbing her, but she ran away before I could. I must say, I had a feeling she was up to something and hoped she'd run away to the fae realm so I could find a way in. They say we can't enter there, but I have my doubts."

"You allowed her to escape and kept me?" All this time, he'd purposely kept me away from my family. "When I'm not even your blood?" And this proved he smelled the same whether he told the truth or a lie. He could hide his true intentions from everyone.

"Of course. I needed you." He shrugged like it was no big deal. "It worked out for the best. I got to live knowing your mother was out there, thinking you were dead. It made it all worthwhile."

"You bastard." I'd never felt so much hate in my life. "You deserve to burn in Hell."

"Maybe, but I'll rule there same as here." He tilted his head, staring at me. "How did you figure out you weren't mine?"

"When the fae began attacking me." Maybe if I scared him, he would let me leave. "They're trying to kill me and anyone near me."

"Ah, so they found you." He pursed his lips. "That's why you were with that fae girl at school. We noticed her the other day, and they said you were outside her room."

"If I stay here, you could die." The only person he cared about was himself, so maybe this would work.

Tyler didn't flinch. "I'll take the risk. From what I've been told, there's a nearby black magic witch who can spell the house and prevent them from coming in."

My heart dropped. The fae wouldn't come near dark magic. "I'll tell everyone I'm not yours."

"And you think they'll believe you?" He laughed hard, tears coming out of the corners of his eyes. "I killed the witch who cursed you with that hair color."

"She was innocent, wasn't she?" My heart dropped. "The witch didn't do it to Roxy, did she?"

"Oh, she did, but because I made her." He grinned. "She didn't expect me to lock her up, but I couldn't risk her telling others that I'd wreaked havoc on that family. Her father was rallying people to rebut me as alpha, so I had to take matters into my own hands. A wolf with strange hair is no good for anyone. When you were born with pink hair, it gave me the perfect excuse to kill her without anyone giving me flak. I righted the wrongs of the witch for our pack, making me more of a leader in the pack's eyes, despite your strangeness."

My whole world had shattered in one sitting. He'd known all along and manipulated everyone, and still, he'd somehow come out on top.

"In a way." He patted my arm. "Avenging you and killing the witch was what saved me and got me where I am today." He lifted a hand. "Okay, so that isn't what I did, but it's what everyone thinks."

"You won't get away with it," I said breathlessly.

"I disagree." He waved his hands around the room. "I already have, and by mating you off to Brock, I'll have the money and backing I need to take over the entire country. And then, when you give birth, I'll use the child as well."

"I will never be a pawn." I needed him to see how much I despised him.

"You've always been a pawn." He turned his back to me and headed to the door. "Sadie, why don't you lie down and get some rest? You look tired." He glanced over his shoulder. "We don't need you looking bad for Brock." He walked out the door and shut it, leaving me alone in the awful room.

I wanted to crumble ... to fall ... to cry. But I pushed that down, refusing to stumble. I would stand tall and be the alpha my pack deserved. Tyler was going down. I'd rip his empire away from him. And when he begged me to stop and have mercy, I'd make sure he took his last breath.

Footsteps sounded out in the hallway, heading in this direction. They weren't heavy enough to be Tyler. Maybe someone was just walking by.

When the doorknob jiggled and the overwhelmingly thick scent of musk hit me, I knew who it was.

God, I couldn't get a break.

The door opened, revealing Brock, Tommy, and another guy. What the hell did they want?

"Looks like you and Tyler caught up." Brock didn't bother trying to sound concerned. "Is everything okay?"

"No, it's not." I was done playing games. I hated each and every one of them with a passion like no other. "Why can't you let me be?"

"Because I need you to get what I really want." Brock motioned for the two idiots to follow him. "You're gorgeous, and we'll have strong pups, so it's not like you're a hardship ... once you change your attitude."

"I will never change my attitude." I should have locked her in, but my wolf was raging as much as my human side. "I will never mate with you. I'd rather watch you bleed out and die."

"Damn," Tommy stuttered beside him. "She means it."

"Oh, I know," Brock said. He must have commanded them through his pack link because the weird guy and Tommy grabbed my arms and jerked me onto the bed. They held me down by my arms and legs.

I bucked, desperate to get out. I wasn't sure what they had planned, but if they needed to restrain me, it couldn't be anything good. However, I was at their mercy.

Brock leaned over my body. "There's only one thing I can do to turn this all around."

Heart racing, I shook my head. "You wouldn't." This was what the mating ceremony was for.

"Oh, I would." He lowered his head to my neck, and his teeth extended.

No, this couldn't happen.

ABOUT THE AUTHOR

Jen L. Grey is a *USA Today* Bestselling Author who writes Paranormal Romance, Urban Fantasy, and Fantasy genres.

Jen lives in Tennessee with her husband, two daughters, and two miniature Australian Shepherd. Before she began writing, she was an avid reader and enjoyed being involved in the indie community. Her love for books eventually led her to writing. For more information, please visit her website and sign up for her newsletter.

Check out my future projects and book signing events at my website.
www.jenlgrey.com

ALSO BY JEN L. GREY

The Wolf Born Trilogy

Hidden Mate

Blood Secrets

Awakened Magic

The Marked Wolf Trilogy

Moon Kissed

Chosen Wolf

Broken Curse

Wolf Moon Academy Trilogy

Shadow Mate

Blood Legacy

Rising Fate

The Royal Heir Trilogy

Wolves' Queen

Wolf Unleashed

Wolf's Claim

Bloodshed Academy Trilogy

Year One

Year Two

Year Three

The Half-Breed Prison Duology (Same World As Bloodshed Academy)

Hunted

Cursed

The Artifact Reaper Series

Reaper: The Beginning

Reaper of Earth

Reaper of Wings

Reaper of Flames

Reaper of Water

Stones of Amaria (Shared World)

Kingdom of Storms

Kingdom of Shadows

Kingdom of Ruins

Kingdom of Fire

The Pearson Prophecy

Dawning Ascent

Enlightened Ascent

Reigning Ascent

Stand Alones

Death's Angel

Rising Alpha

CPSIA information can be obtained
at www.ICGtesting.com
Printed in the USA
LVHW101142170722
723701LV00019B/164

9 781955 616010